A Ripple of Murders

A RIPPLE
OF MURDERS

John Wainwright

ST. MARTIN'S
NEW YORK

Printed in Hong Kong

Library of Congress Catalog Card Number 78-66406

First published in the United States of America in 1979

ISBN: 0-312-68243-3

FRIDAY – JULY 29th

12.30 p.m. – 4 p.m.

The shot was a little out. No more than an inch, or so; it had been aimed at the heart and (as so often happens) the killer had estimated the heart as being fractionally too far left of breast-centre.

But, it was near enough. It did not kill outright, but it eventually extinguished life.

There was the usual reaction. A moment of stunned disbelief on the part of fellow-pedestrians, followed by a milling and a chattering – an anger and an outrage – and (as far as the victim was concerned) a nightmare closing in of too many people all over-anxious to help. Before consciousness left him, the shot youth experienced growing pain and mounting panic; a pain which was like a furnace in his chest, radiating pulsating heat to every corner of his body, and a panic originating from a closing sea of wide-eyed faces, each distorted by shock and concern.

The squad car arrived as the rear doors of the ambulance were being slammed shut. There was obvious urgency, therefore the police driver took up position ahead of the ambulance and, with flashing light and sounding gong, carved a racing path through the midday traffic towards Lessford General Infirmary.

The Infirmary machine was waiting; the porters, the nurses, the duty medics. Expertise, combined with speed, had the youth out of the ambulance, on to a trolley,

5

along the corridors and into an emergency examination room within two minutes.

It was all wasted.

Less than thirty minutes later, when the sheet-covered body of the murdered youth was wheeled to the mortuary in the basement of Lessford General Infirmary, a cheap, tie-on label was attached to the left ankle. The label read 'D.O.A.' – Dead On Arrival. . . .

Gilliant took a deep breath, and muttered, 'Nice.'

Actually, he meant 'nasty', but that is the way the English language is screwed around, even by well-educated people, especially when those people are straddle-legged over a particularly uncomfortable barrel.

'Who's at the scene?' he asked.

'Preston.' 157084

Gilliant compressed his lips, nodded and squeezed what small personal relief he could from the answer.

Sullivan added, 'Preston can hold the fort, pending things getting under way.'

'Dick.' Gilliant looked up at his deputy chief constable, with the eyes of a man carrying back-breaking responsibility. The words held a sigh, as he said, 'Preston can't carry the can. That belongs to this office. *The Tribune* asked our advice. We gave it. The wrong advice.'

'Not necessarily,' argued Sullivan.

'Are you prepared to split hairs with the next-of-kin?'

'I'll see 'em.'

'Oh, for God's sake . . .'

'I'll see 'em,' repeated Sullivan, doggedly. 'I'll tell 'em about the letter. That we told *The Tribune* not to publish it. And *why* we told *The Tribune* not to publish it. It was a responsible decision. A lad's been murdered. It's a pity, and I'm sorry and whoever did the killing will be caught. I'll see to that, personally. But, it was *still* a responsible decision.'

'Would you think so?' asked Gilliant, softly.

'If you mean . . .'

'Steve?'

And, that was the rub; the point at which being a policeman, and being a father, produced a conflict of loyalties. Had it been Steve . . . By God, had it been Steve he'd have had somebody's guts in the nearest frying pan. Had it been Steve. And, had he *not* been a copper.

Gilliant said, 'Sit down, Dick. He is coming across, immediately. And Bear. Then, between us, we'll decide some course of action.'

Sullivan grunted, chose one of a scattering of spare chairs and lowered himself on to its leather-covered seat.

For a moment (and, probably, for the first time in his life) Sullivan felt a sympathy for Gilliant; a sympathy which almost amounted to a feeling of pity. The man was cold, unemotional, near-unapproachable and, when necessary, almost fanatically ruthless . . . but, by Christ, what a load to carry! It had been heavy enough in the old days; in the once-upon-a-time days, when Lessford, a city of three-quarters of a million souls, had had its own police force, headed by a younger Gilliant; when Sullivan, as a uniformed chief superintendent, had blitzed the tearaways of North End, the toughest division in the city. Yes, even when he'd been bumped up to assistant chief constable (crime), life and policing (which *was* his life) had been worth the candle; Gilliant had been the cool, unflappable figure in the background; the boss who expected results and who, as long as he got those results, argued the pro's and con's with the Watch Committee and kept pipsqueak officialdom out of everybody's hair.

Until, that is, some bloody fool at Whitehall had doodled a line on a map, and created the Lessford Metropolitan Police District. Jesus Christ! Somebody should tell somebody the facts of life; that 'big' is not another name for 'beautiful'.

Gilliant had been offered the skippership of the new M.P.D., and had accepted. The old Lessford police area – plus the police area of the twin town of Bordfield – plus a damn great hunk of the old county constabulary area. A million and a half acres . . . as near as dammit is to swearing. A population topping the two million mark, policed by just over six thousand coppers; and many of those coppers still owing subconscious allegiance to their old mobs. Three forces, suddenly lumped together to form one bumper bundle.

He (Sullivan) had had another kick up the ladder of promotion; to the post of deputy chief constable, along with 'Winnie' Bear. And assistant chief constables and heads of C.I.D. by the bucketful . . . or, so it seemed. All chiefs, no Indians. All sheriffs, no cowboys. That's how Sullivan saw it. Like TV cops-and-robbers; only mindless slobs under the rank of chief inspector.

But they weren't and never had been. But it was what they were rapidly becoming. The image was there, and reality was gradually accepting the image as the truth. Men were losing their pride; their force – the force they'd *had* pride in – had been destroyed, and this socking great M.P.D. thing couldn't command the same parochial loyalty. It was unwieldy. It was without heart. It couldn't be handled.

But Gilliant was expected to handle it.

And now this.

Gilliant frowned at his own thoughts and rubbed the side of his jaw with the fingertips of his left hand. Sullivan watched and felt sympathy, amounting to pity, for his chief.

A knock on the office door brought Gilliant's thoughts to earth.

8

He lowered his hand, and called, 'Come in.'

The door opened and Deputy Chief Constable Bear entered the office, followed by Walter Kingsley, the editor of *The Lessford and Bordfield Tribune*.

The killer was neither surprised nor disappointed. This first shooting was part of his calculations; it would need one – probably even two – before he was no longer dismissed as a crank. After that he would be feared. And, after *that*, he would be obeyed.

Thereafter he would become progressively richer, until he was very rich. Then the killings would cease. He would emigrate. To Canada, he thought – he had almost decided that it would be Canada, British Columbia if he had a choice, and he certainly *would* have a choice – and there he would end his days in quiet luxury. Nothing ostentatious. Nothing to arouse the curiosity of officialdom. A nice house, a few carefully chosen friends and the wherewithal to enjoy the moderation he longed for. The moderation refused him in this crazy age of industrial confrontation.

He was a widower in his mid-fifties. In his life he'd loved, and would only love, one wife and for three years he'd been a very lonely man. He'd served a careful apprenticeship, prior to Hitler's war and, after a four-year stint in the R.A.S.C., he'd returned to his lathe, with dreams of starting up a small, high-class engineering firm.

It could, so easily, have been a success. Indeed, it *was* a success – for a decade it expanded, slowly but very surely, and for two years the firm's bank balance had been firmly in the black – until 1957.

Precision engineering. How could any man have forecast that it was possible to be *too* good? That ultra-accuracy in the shaping of metal was something a slipshod world couldn't afford? Or that the warning by the World Health Organisation of the effects of radiation would reach out and touch a tiny firm on the outskirts of Lessford?

The warning had come on March 11th. By April 3rd, the British Labour Party was calling for the abolition of H-bomb tests. May 15th saw the first British H-bomb exploded in the Central Pacific, near Christmas Island, and June 19th saw the completion of the whole test programme.

Since then . . . nothing!

The ridiculous thing was that he – even *he*, the boss – hadn't known what it was they were making. Just one tiny, delicately turned piece of special metal, manufactured to precise specifications; a single part of the thousands of parts necessary to produce a hydrogen blast. Probably not even part of the bomb itself; probably part of the exploding mechanism; probably a piece of the involved instrumentation with which the explosion was measured.

He didn't know.

He'd never known.

The only thing he'd known was that, without H-bomb tests, the government contract had been cancelled, and nothing had been found with which to fill the gap. Precision engineering had had its day; that, or what call there still was on precision engineering, was already being met by existing firms.

And because he'd refused to lower his standards the profits had gone and, after the profits, the firm. Gradually. Over the years. The long and lost fight to prevent a 'closed shop'. And thereafter wage demand after wage demand; outrageous demands which couldn't possibly be met. Strikes and, with the strikes, the loss of what little business they had left. Then, the final ignominy; bankruptcy. The end of the firm and the fouling of a dream.

Mabel had gone, before then; before the greed of

other men had beaten him to the gutter. A heartbreak, which had been a strange and peculiar blessing; that she who had had so much trust had not lived to witness the fiscal treachery of so-called friends.

Thus the killer.

A good man soured and perhaps driven a little mad. But a wise man who was neither surprised nor disappointed; a man who knew it would take one – probably even two – killings before he was no longer dismissed as a crank.

As Bear read a photostat of the letter, Gilliant said, 'Only three of us knew. Mr. Kingsley, Mr. Sullivan and myself.'

'Four of us,' Kingsley corrected Gilliant. 'My secretary opens my mail. She read the letter. Naturally.'

'Now five of us,' murmured Gilliant.

Bear read the photostat.

It is my intention to kill a pedestrian on the streets of Lessford, on Friday 29th July. I can be stopped by the insertion of a small ad. in the Personal Column of The Lessford and Bordfield Tribune. *The ad. will read 'J.D. Message received. All arrangements have been made'.*

The insertion must be made in the edition of Thursday 28th July.

The arrangements referred to are as follows. The sum of £10,000, in used and unmarked Bank of England notes, none of whose denomination must be greater than £10, to be held ready at your office. Thereafter, my telephoned instructions to be followed to the letter.

In the event of you not agreeing to these terms, do not insert the small ad.

In the event of you notifying the police of this letter and/or inserting the ad. with the intention of trapping me, I will kill two pedestrians on the streets of Lessford, on Saturday, 30th July.

J.D.

Bear looked up from the photostat, and breathed, 'Christ!'

'The letter, the envelope.' Gilliant waved a hand, and answered unasked questions. 'We've had them both through the forensic science machine. The paper, "Plus Fabric" bond, made by the Reed group. Good quality paper, but not uncommon. The envelope, P.O.P. size, "Clyde" white laid – one of the "river" series – made by the Wiggins Teape firm. Again, good quality, but not uncommon. The stamp, first class, from a sheet. Presumably sold over a Post Office counter. Posted at Lessford Central Post Office, and franked with the two o'clock, afternoon collection, on the Wednesday. The twenty-seventh. The type, small pica, the letter and the envelope typed on the same machine. The envelope, incidentally, was addressed to Mr. Kingsley, by name. After that, it's mainly guesswork. We think an Olympia machine, old or misused. Six of the letters are badly out of alignment. That's about all.' Gilliant paused, then ended, 'Mr. Kingsley did the right thing. He brought the letter round here. We gave advice.'

'We?' Bear's voice was low.

'Mr. Sullivan and I.'

'Not very good advice.' Bear made no attempt to hide his derision.

'Hey, Winnie, look . . .'

'*Don't* call me "Winnie", Mr. Sullivan.' Bear turned on his companion deputy chief constable. 'This thing.' Bear tapped the photostat with the nail of a forefinger. 'Some lunatic writes a letter, saying he's going to commit murder. Tells you where. Tells you when. And you do damn-all about it. Nothing! You just let him go ahead. Christ . . . what sort of coppers *are* you?'

'It might have been a hoax,' said Gilliant, gently. 'On the face of things . . .'

'It *wasn't* a hoax.'

'All right . . . Deputy Chief Constable Bear.' Sullivan's voice carried the indignation of which only the guilt of miscalculation is capable. 'It wasn't a hoax. We all know that. *Now*. But, how many crackpot letters do we receive? How many threats that don't mean a damn thing? This could have been one of 'em. One more. We thought it was.'

'You could have put the small ad. in the . . .'

'And, if we had?'

'There wouldn't have been a killing.'

'No. Two killings.'

'If you were so damn sure it was a hoax . . .'

'You,' said Sullivan harshly, 'want to make your mind up which horse you're riding, Bear. Hoax or no hoax. Take it seriously and there's a killing. Insert the ad., and there's two killings. If it's a hoax . . . nothing. It was a calculated risk. We took it.'

'I hope you can sleep nights,' sneered Bear.

'Gentlemen.' Gilliant raised his hands a few inches from the desk top. 'The decision – the final decision – was mine. A wrong decision. I accept that, and make no attempt at excusing it. Had I taken the letter seriously – had I advised the insertion of the paragraph in the Personal Column – we might well have saved a life. I accept that, too. But, to insert the paragraph would have been little more than pointless, without ten thousand pounds at our disposal. Had we assumed it was *not* a hoax – had we gone along with the instructions in the letter – we would have needed the money, if only as a back-up to any scheme we might have worked out. In case the scheme went wrong . . . and schemes *do* go wrong. If it *had* gone wrong, there would have been a second killing. That possibility, too, had to be taken into consideration. The killer – "J.D.", whoever he is – might well have been ten thousand pounds richer and still kill again, tomorrow. Two victims, not one. That was the choice. Nothing, if it was a hoax. One murder, if it wasn't a hoax, and the paragraph wasn't inserted. Two murders, if it wasn't a hoax, if the paragraph *had* been inserted, and if any scheme we might have thought up had gone wrong. Mr. Sullivan has called it a calculated risk. That's exactly what it was. None, one or two . . . we couldn't possibly risk two.'

Bear's expression showed a degree of mollification; mollification, mixed with some doubt, but without the furious disgust it had carried a few moments before.

He looked at Gilliant, Sullivan and Kingsley in turn then said, 'And now, what?'

Before either of the other two could speak, Kingsley said, 'And now, we're going to publish the letter. Front page, centre, in tomorrow's edition. Plus the decision we made. *We* made . . . I associate myself with that decision, without qualification. The public have the right to know.'

By mid-afternoon 'the public' were being pushed around a little. Preston – Detective Superintendent Preston – was the pusher-in-chief.

Preston was an officer for whom the amalgamation shake-up had done nothing; one of the few senior policemen who had not benefited. He'd been a detective superintendent in the old Lessford City force. He was still a detective superintendent in the new Lessford Metropolitan Police District.

Other men had prospered as a result of the reorganisation. Rucker, for example. Oh, yes, *Rucker*. Rucker had been a mere detective chief inspector, in the old force. The word 'mere', of course, being a comparative adjec-

14

tive, but nevertheless a man to whom Preston had given orders in the old force. But, in the *new* force. For some reason, best known to the law-enforcement Gods, in this piss-arsed, M.P.D. balls-up, Rucker had performed a neat little leap-frog in the promotion race; from detective chief inspector to detective chief superintendent and to head of Lessford Region C.I.D. Which meant that Rucker now gave the orders, and Preston obeyed them. And nobody, but *nobody*, gave orders quite like Rucker.

This, then, was a burden (one of many) which Preston was required to carry. An invisible burden; a burden born of 'police politics'; a burden not known, and not understood, by the aforementioned 'public', many of whom still subscribed to the hoary, our-policemen-are-wonderful line of thought.

We-ell, maybe they were . . . some of 'em. But Preston was only 'wonderful' in the way a charging rhino might be thought wonderful. Deadly. Destructive. And extra-ordinarily ill-tempered.

And, most of all, unnecessarily loud.

'You were there,' he bawled.

'Yes.' The proprietor almost ducked, as the decibels assaulted his eardrums.

'At the door of this bloody dress shop of yours.'

'Boutique,' murmured the proprietor.

'Eh?'

'It's a boutique. It isn't a dress shop.'

'You sell dresses, don't you?'

'Yes, but . . .'

'It's a bloody dress shop.'

The proprietor sighed and lifted his shoulders, resignedly.

Preston shouted, 'You were at the door.'

'Yes.'

'And laddo was passing? Right?'

'Y-you mean the . . .'

'Laddo.'

'The – the victim?'

'Laddo,' insisted Preston. 'He was passing. He ended up at your ankles.'

'Ye-es.'

'So, c'mon, where did the blasted shot come from?'

'I don't know.'

'Where did it sound to come from?'

'I-I didn't hear anything.'

'A gun.' Preston shoved his jaw forward, aggressively. 'We're talking about a gun, lad. Not a pea-shooter. Not a catapult. A gun, and guns go bang. They make a noise. Now – c'mon – you must have heard summat.'

'No. I'm sorry . . .'

'Judas priest! *Summat.*'

'N-no. The traffic. I wasn't – wasn't particularly listening. It's not that . . .'

'Are you bloody deaf?' roared Preston.

'If not,' a voice purred, 'he soon will be.'

'Eh?'

Preston turned. His speed of turn was such that he almost tripped over his own ankles. He knew the voice; knew that he'd see that everlasting curve of contempt on the lips; knew that the eyes would, as always, view him with more disdain than seemed humanly possible.

Rucker had arrived. Preston's bowl of mortification was filled and ran over.

Nor, must it be understood, were the grandees of the Lessford Metropolitan Police District the only personages getting warm around the collar. The law-enforcement commonalty – the proletariat, the great unwashed of the forensic world – had their own troubles, and troubles peculiar to themselves.

Murder. As a crime, it keeps the scribblers occupied, lines their pockets and, with luck, keeps one section of the reading public wide-eyed and wondering. Fictitious murder, that is; impossible murder, committed within the confines of hermetically sealed rooms; bloodless, painless and, above all else, quite 'acceptable' murder; murder which, within the next two hundred pages, or so, will be solved with a certain gay panache, by the smiling, handsome amateur, while the local, flat-footed gendarmerie are still struggling to lace up their size tens.

Thus fairy-tale murder. 157084

But the *real* thing . . . oh, no!

The real thing was as glamorous as an abattoir; as entertaining as a hanging-shed; as amusing as a firing squad. The real thing presupposed that some lunatic had nudged God from His pedestal; had taken over the business of life-and-death decision-making.

The real thing meant work in large lumps. It meant aching feet, frayed tempers and dry throats, asking the same question umpteen dozen times without once getting a straight answer. The P.B.I. – the police constables and the detective constables, the uniformed sergeants and the detective sergeants – made up the slave-labour necessary in order that the base of that pyramid of enquiry known as 'A Murder Hunt' might have firm foundations. Theirs was the in-bulk work. The collection and submission of what might eventually run into hundreds, and possibly thousands, of piffling, unimportant statements; unimportant in that they added nothing to the enquiry, but *very* important in that they eliminated the maker of the statement from any list of people who *might* add something to the enquiry. This monumental clearing away of dross had a fancy name. It was known as 'House-to-House Enquiries'.

And even this was a misnomer. The shooting had taken place in King Street, and King Street had no houses as such. A handful of flats above some of the many shops but, apart from these, it was a place of offices, emporiums, chain-stores and the Lessford Odeon Cinema.

Nevertheless, the flatfeet and the jacks trudged their weary round. Asked questions. Noted answers. And wondered why the hell the poor guy had been shot, in the first place.

The detective sergeant was accompanied by one of the 'ancient mariners' of the uniformed branch. The D.S. was a young chap, therefore, regardless of his rank, he tacitly acknowledged the know-how of his aged companion constable. Experience carried its own authority.

The P.C. said, 'You stand at this counter all day, luv?'

The middle-aged lady clerk, employee of the Provincial Building Society, preened herself a little. It was many a long month since a strange man had used even a mild term of endearment when addressing her.

She smiled, and said, 'Yes. Most of the day.'

'You'll have a good view of the street through the window.'

The P.C. jerked his head towards the area of plate-glass which separated the pavement from the carpeted floor leading up to the counter.

'Yes.' She nodded, then added, 'When I'm not busy with customers, of course.'

'Aye – we-ell – of course, you'll be busy most o' the time. That's understandable.' The elderly copper used all the age-old tricks of pseudo-charm, subtle buttering-up and quasi-sympathy. He allowed the wraith of an embarrassed smile to touch his lips, as he said, 'Y'know why we're here o' course.'

'The – er – the shooting.'

'Aye.'

'Terrible. When they told me, I could hardly believe it.'

'Don't worry, luv,' soothed the elderly copper. 'We'll get him.'

'Oh . . . I'm sure.'

'Just that – y'know. . .' The elderly copper moved his hands, almost apologetically. 'You didn't happen to see anything, did you?'

'Me?' The lady clerk looked shocked.

'No, not the shooting, luv.' The elderly copper calmed the rising agitation. 'You couldn't have seen that. Not from here. But, y'see, whoever did it might have passed the window.'

'I–I–I wouldn't . . . How would *I* . . . ?'

'Well,' explained the elderly copper, patiently. 'He had a gun, y'see. He had to have a gun. Some sorta rifle, we think.'

'I – I didn't see anybody with a . . .'

'Or summat he might be carrying it in.'

'I – I can't help you. Really I can't.' The lady clerk was beginning to be flustered. 'I – I'd like to help you. I *would* help you, if I could. But . . .'

'A rifle,' repeated the elderly copper, gently. 'It's, y'know, a bit clumsy to cart around, in the normal course o' events. In a bag, maybe. Some sorta longish bag. Summat like that. Summat you'd notice.'

'No.' The lady clerk shook her head. 'I didn't see anybody carrying a bag.' She paused, frowned, then added, 'But . . .'

'Yes, luv?'

'It wouldn't have to be a bag. Would it?'

'No,' agreed the elderly copper.

'Only . . .' Again she hesitated, then said, 'I saw the window-cleaner. Just before it happened. I *think* it was just before it happened.'

'Go on,' encouraged the elderly copper, quietly.

'Well,' said the lady clerk, 'he has a hand-cart. For his ladders, I mean. A little hand-cart. With sides. I – I suppose he could . . .'

'Aye.' The elderly copper nodded, solemnly.

'I – I don't want to get anybody into trouble. It's not that I . . .'

'He'll wanna help, too,' the elderly copper assured her. 'Now, d'you know his name? This window-cleaner chap?'

'Er – William . . . no *Williams*. With an "s". He has it painted, on the sides. The sides of the hand-cart, I mean.'

'Champion.' The elderly copper beamed his approval. He glanced at the D.S., and said, 'Now, then. Just give this young chap your name, and address. That's all, to say you've been seen, then you won't be bothered again. Age? I'd say "over twenty-one", that's good enough.' His eyes twinkled a little, as he added, 'You *are* over twenty-one, aren't you?'

She blushed as she nodded.

'Champion,' repeated the elderly copper. 'I wish everybody was as easy to talk to.'

The young detective sergeant wished something, too. He wished he had the elderly copper's interviewing technique.

By four o'clock, Gilliant, Sullivan and Bear had agreed upon the general direction of the enquiry. Kingsley had returned to the slightly less hectic world of *The Lessford and Bordfield Tribune*. Under Gilliant's persuasion, the two deputy chief constables had for the moment kissed and made up, figuratively speaking. The trio were still in Gilliant's office. Sullivan was smoking his pipe, Bear was smoking a cigarette, and both of them were listening to the words of the man at the top.

Gilliant was saying, '. . . it seems, therefore, that we're about to have a ton of bricks dropped on the back of our necks. I don't blame Kingsley. His priorities aren't ours. But when he publishes that letter, we can expect trouble. Whoever "J.D." is . . .'

'John Doe,' said Bear, suddenly.

'What?' Gilliant paused, in mid-sentence, to stare at his deputy.

'John Doe,' repeated Bear. 'The Yanks use the name more than we do. The imaginary citizen. The legal fiction. I doubt whether his initials *are* "J" and "D".'

'Why not?' grunted Sullivan.

'He hides everything else, but gives us his initials?' The spat of mutual annoyance between the two deputy chief constables had not quite cleared.

Sullivan growled, 'He's not chancing much.'

'Nevertheless . . .' Gilliant nodded slowly. 'I think John Doe. Not because that's his name, but because we *need* a name. It makes him less of a shadow. Something we can chase.'

'We'd be kidding ourselves.'

'Very well, *let's* kid ourselves.' Gilliant silenced Sullivan's objections with a quick, tight smile. 'John Doe will read that letter, when it's published in the *Tribune*. He'll know *we* know. So will a lot of other people, including every policeman in the force. And questions will be asked. Very awkward questions.'

'Very pertinent questions,' said Bear.

'Probably.' Gilliant compressed his lips, then went on. 'The letter, itself – its contents – give reason enough. A man's been killed. One man, not two. It's poor consolation, but it's reason enough for keeping quiet.'

'And now?' asked Bear.

'We sweat it out, Mr. Bear. What else. This – er – John Doe has carried out his threat. He's killed one pedestrian. As far as he's concerned the *Tribune* didn't tell the police. There's nothing to suggest they did. The publication of the letter? That's something he could have expected. Especially after the murder. We can only hope that he keeps it at one, until he contacts the *Tribune* again.'

'It's a pattern,' said Sullivan, heavily.

'Quite. Let's hope he sticks to the pattern. He might give himself away.'

Bear murmured, 'Why not produce the ten thousand quid, then grab him, when he collects it?'

'Just like that,' said Sullivan, sourly. 'Ten thousand smackers. Loose change.'

'When compared with human life,' argued Bear.

Gilliant said, 'We can get the money. Any one of the big four banks will co-operate.'

'For a spot of buckshee publicity.'

'Mr. Sullivan.' Gilliant's tone warned of a shortening of patience. 'I don't give a penny damn whether it's publicity, or whether it's philanthropy. If this John Doe character contacts the *Tribune* again, if he demands his pound of flesh, we'll at least go through the motions. We now know he isn't some practical joker. We know he means business. It isn't much, but at least we know *that*. We need a war council. Six o'clock in the Recreation Room. Set it up as the Operations Centre. And I want every senior officer present, from superintendent up. C.I.D. *and* uniformed. I have a gut-feeling, gentlemen. And I don't like it.'

It was not that the manager of the Odeon was anti-police, not that in any shape or form, at least not *much*. But (to use an expression) times were hard and getting harder. This picture palace, for example. He could remember the days when the customers queued, three-deep, for more than a hundred yards. Every Saturday night and, when there was a good film showing, every night of the week. When Messrs. Bogart, Tracy and Gable, and mesdames Davis, Crawford and Loy pulled them in by the thousand. The great days of the motion picture, my friend, when Hollywood was the escape route to Never-Never-Land; when Cooper said 'Yup' and every female in the audience was ready to throw herself at his feet; when Stanwyk fluttered those eyelashes and every red-blooded male felt the sudden surge of extra adrenalin.

But today?

Odeon One and Odeon Two, for God's sake! Two films, two screens, to pull in a fraction of the old audiences. And *what* films! Skin-flicks; soft porn, for old goats who were past it, and young would-be rams who didn't yet know how the hell to make it. That or disaster movies; ships turning turtle, sky-scrapers blazing like torches, man-eating sharks and woman-lusting gorillas. The whole damn world was going kinky, but that wasn't his fault; his job was to screen what the public wanted to see. Not to *like* it. Just to *screen* it. The bosses who ran the circuit expected him to make money, and what happened? *Last Tango in Paris. The Clockwork Orange. Deep Throat.* Some holier-than-thou law – some sanctimonious watchdog of public morals – had dropped the boom on all three films. Leeds? . . . sure. Bradford . . . why not? But Lessford? . . . not on your nelly.

So the customers had taken a bus ride and the takings had dropped one more notch.

The manager of the Odeon was therefore no law-fan and, although he was not anti-police, the law (as far as he was concerned) equated with large men wearing dark blue uniforms. Hence his attitude to the uniformed sergeant who asked the questions.

He said, 'No. I don't stand in the foyer all day. I'm the manager. I have to keep my eyes open. Everywhere. Both auditoriums. I walk miles.'

'But most of the time,' insisted the sergeant.

'No. Not most of the time. There's a projectionist in Number Two Box. A box Brownie . . . that's about *his* limit.'

23

'At the time of the shooting?' suggested the sergeant, hopefully.

'I was in Number One. Some young hooligan was throwing orange peel around.'

'Oh!'

'By the time I got back here it had all happened. The ambulance had just arrived.'

'Notice anybody nipping in?' asked the P.C. who accompanied the sergeant.

'Nipping in?' The manager looked almost offended.

'Into the cinema?'

'They don't "nip in". They pay or they don't *get* in.'

'All right. Somebody . . .'

'I've already asked. Nobody bought a ticket fifteen minutes before or fifteen minutes after it happened. We didn't open till noon. We were still showing the adverts.'

'Not many customers?' The sergeant made the question a vehicle for sympathy.

'Pensioners,' complained the manager. 'Cheap rate until five. I swear . . . we don't even cover overheads.'

The P.C. asked, 'What about the toilets?'

'Sure. They use the toilets.' The manager looked nonplussed.

'No. I mean other people. Not customers.'

'It's not a public . . .'

'It's sometimes used as such,' smiled the P.C.

'Is it, by gum?'

'Didn't you know?'

'No. I didn't know. If I'd known . . .'

'I've used 'em myself,' confessed the P.C.

'Y'mean, without paying? Without buying a ticket?'

The P.C. said, 'I'm not going to buy a ticket just for a quick slash.'

'You've got a nerve.' The manager glared.

'So,' observed the sergeant, 'it can be done.'

'Ask your pal.' The manager retreated behind a façade

of offended outrage. 'He seems to know more about the toilet arrangements here than I do.'

'You,' said the sergeant, flatly, 'were busy chasing kids throwing orange peel . . . right?'

It was that sort of interview; a get-nowhere-learn-nothing interview on the face of it. Two not-too-enthusiastic interviewers, and one mildly biased interviewee. That they touched a truth, without knowing it, was nobody's fault.

The killer, the man the police had already christened John Doe, unzipped the British Airways handbag and removed the various parts of his killing-tool.

It was a rifle and yet, it was *not* a rifle. It was certainly not *one* rifle. The breech and the chamber were from an ancient Short Lee-Enfield, adapted to fire a single round of .303 Army ammunition. The barrel was from a Weatherby Mark V, .300, re-bored to an extra three thou., then shortened to less than nine inches. The trigger action was from a Browning Mauser, and the stock was manufactured from tubular steel, with a concave shoulder-plate. The telescopic sight was a Leupold M7-4x, with a Detacho-Mount locking device, altered to cope with this most peculiar of weapons.

By stretching the meaning of the phrase to near-breaking-point, it might have been possible to use the American vernacular and to have called the rifle a 'zip-gun'. Zip-guns were home-made weapons and this was a home-made weapon. Zip-guns were built up from odds and ends of discarded ironmongery, plus bits and pieces of otherwise lawful merchandise : the same could be said of John Doe's rifle. Zip-guns were made to fire one shot then had to be manually re-loaded, as with the rifle. Zip-guns were *very* unlawful and no authority in the civilised world would have granted a firearms certificate in relation to the weapon manufactured by John Doe.

A zip-gun then, but *what* a zip-gun.

It had taken the man more than three years to collect the various thrown-away parts; to plan and draw the proposed weapon, then to turn it and fashion it in the tiny workshop, at the rear of his garage, at home. The gun itself was ample proof of his skill in the working of metals. It really *was* 'hand made'. Tailored to take the two dozen or so .303 rounds of ammunition, souvenirs of his war service. Made to dismantle into pieces, none of which exceeded nine inches in length; cunningly constructed to screw and lock into position with, as a last refinement, a flash-eliminator-cum-silencer – a superbly made, interior baffled gadget, of his own design – which added a further six inches to the barrel, did nothing to interfere with the telescopic sight, but balanced the completed rifle beautifully.

A zip-gun, if you will. But also a purpose-built weapon which only a craftsman could produce.

The killer placed each part of the rifle on the yellow duster which was spread on the bench of his workshop. He cleaned and oiled each part, very carefully. Then he stored the parts away in their various hiding places. In the base of the lathe; in the tool chest along with the files, the scrapers and the calipers; in the recess, behind the fuse-box; on the ledge, beneath the top of the workbench. Ten different places; each place safe and secret; each place carefully chosen and away from its neighbour.

He took the empty cartridge-case, which he had removed from the chamber of his gun, and fitted it into the teeth of his lathe. He pressed a switch and picked up a hacksaw. Within minutes the brass of the cartridge-case had been scored and distorted; no comparison-microscope on earth could have linked *that* cartridge-case with the breech, the chamber or the striking-pin of *his* rifle. He stopped the lathe, removed the cartridge-case, then hammered it into a shapeless mass before dropping it into the box containing filings and metal shavings.

A careful man. A thinking man. More than that, a thoughtful man.

Back in the house he lifted the telephone receiver from its rest, dialled a number, then held a gentle conversation with his daughter.

'How goes the day, Kim?'

'Steady, Pop. Nothing to shout about. Just steady.'

'Sleeping?'

'I read a lot. It makes me tired . . . eventually.'

'You keep off those pills, sweetheart.'

'Sure.'

'You hear me?'

'I hear you, Pop.'

'I mean it.'

'Sure.'

'You should get out more.'

'It wouldn't help.'

'Meet nice people.'

'Where do I find nice people, Pop?'

'Don't be cynical, sweetheart. Not at your age.'

'That? From you?'

'You're a generation, Kim. We need people like you.'

'And Sam?'

'Sam was right. He went about it the wrong way, that's all.'

'Pop, that's just an excuse.'

'He was right, sweetheart. Don't ever think he wasn't right.'

'So right. That's why he's inside.'

'Honey, he's no criminal.'

'That, too, is why he's inside.'

'You have more brains than that, Kim.'

'Pop, you're a good man.'

'I once thought so.'

27

'A *good* man, Pop. Believe me.'

'Like the man said . . . "I have a dream." '

'I love you, Pop.'

'Yeah. Me, too, sweetheart. Maybe that's enough.'

'Pop, why do they screw us so?'

A conversation, carried along telephone wires. A daily exchange of paternal and daughterly affection, between a killer and his only child.

The man never once thought of himself as a killer, as a murderer, as a taker of innocent life. What he had done, little more than three hours previously, was not merely dismissed, it was never even *there*. There was no feeling of guilt. No sadness. No regret.

It was part of a plan – a plan for personal survival – and the death of strangers was part of that plan. Therefore, strangers must die.

Strangers must die, in order to ensure that he and his daughter and his son-in-law might live.

6 p.m.

The Recreation Room. Sullivan sat on a tubular-steel and canvas chair and killed time by busying himself with his own thoughts.

Recreation Rooms, for example. Why, by all the Gods, should every architect who ever planned a modern nick always include in those plans a 'Recreation Room'? Why the universal belief that coppers (unlike other men) are loth to leave their place of work? Why, *always*, a 'Recreation Room'?

Billiards, snooker, ping-pong, darts? What the hell sort of cockeyed logic argued that a man (or a woman) wanted to tool around with such brands of foolishness, after a hard day's graft? After a hard *night's* graft? Badminton? Netball? They were even dafter; the carefully painted lines on the polished floor had all been wasted. Always would be wasted.

One day the planners would get the message. That by the very nature of their profession coppers worked up to the ear-holes in muck and corruption; that after long hours listening to and witnessing the end-product of man's blind stupidity – *and* rottenness – the last thing any bloke (or lass) wanted to do was hang around the very monument to that end-product, when he could be at his own hearth, with his own family, his own friends.

So this was what every police station Recreation Room was good for, and the *only* thing it was good for. A room big enough to be an Operations Centre, whenever a big crime was committed. A room in which men could be gathered for briefing purposes.

As at this moment.

Sullivan let his eyes wander towards the men who were awaiting the arrival of Gilliant. The big men. The important men. Some of whom were his friends. Some of whom were most decidedly *not* his friends.

Bear. Deputy Chief Constable Bear; the man who level-pegged Sullivan in the hierarchy of the force. A nice chap; maybe *too* nice, *too* decent, for the rank he carried. 'Winnie' to everybody – even the pavement-bashers – and not minding the nickname. 'Winnie', thanks to the writings of A. A. Milne. Bear, *Winnie the Pooh*, 'Winnie', the deputy chief constable.

Dammit, he even looked the part. Stocky; thickset; a little paunchy, with arms and legs on the short side. Rounded, apple-red cheeks at each side of a snub nose. And round brown eyes which refused to hold a grievance for more than a few minutes. Bear was a good man – a good worker – and one of the few (the very few) men Sullivan knew who hadn't become sharp-edged and truculent as a result of years of police authority.

Aye, maybe *too* nice for a deputy chief constable.

Harris, on the other hand . . . Harris had been detective chief superintendent (and Head of C.I.D.) in the old Bordfield City Force. Now with the creation of a provincial M.P.D. Harris was assistant chief constable (crime) for the Bordfield Region. In effect, his old patch, plus a slice of the county area and, as Sullivan knew, that was the only hunk of the Lessford Metropolitan Police District Harris worried about.

Harris was at this senior officers' get-together under sufferance and did little to hide the fact. He had better things to do than monkey around with Lessford crime, even when that crime was murder. Bordfield was *his* manor and, when murder was committed in the Bordfield area, *then* he'd start pulling out the plugs.

Sullivan could follow Harris's thought-process with almost uncanny ease, because he was remarkably like Harris. Too many times in the past he had used the I'm-right-because-I'm-right brand of argument. Too many times his interest in law-enforcement had stopped at Lessford City boundaries. Indeed, at the lesser boundaries of North End Division when he'd been responsible for keeping the lid on that particularly hair-raising portion of Lessford City. And in those days he would have argued that that was the only practical way of bobbying; that, if each man met his own immediate responsibility and met it well, the overall responsibility would, by definition, take care of itself.

It was an old-fashioned view and Harris was an old-fashioned copper. Come to that, so was Sullivan; an old-fashioned copper, forced into a new-fashioned matrix, and sometimes the pressure rubbed him raw.

For that reason Sullivan envied Harris, because Harris had the rank to have his own way, but without the responsibilities which demanded that he *change* his ways.

One day Harris would come an almighty cropper, and then . . .

The door of the Recreation Room opened and Gilliant entered accompanied by Dr. Joseph Carr, M.Sc., Ph.D., director of the Area Forensic Science Laboratory and, because Carr was also attending the conference, every man in the room sat up and took notice.

There was more to this shooting than the usual bang-you're-dead routine.

6.10 p.m.

'You're – er – *were* his friend.' The detective inspector worked hard to combine objectivity and sympathy in their correct measure. 'His girl-friend. Therefore, presumably, his best friend.'

The young woman nodded. She had not yet shed a tear; would not shed a tear until tomorrow. It would take until tomorrow for the numbness to wear off. For reality to rear up and hit her. *Then* she'd weep, but for the moment it was all a mistake. All part of a bad dream. Something she had to go along with but not necessarily believe.

She said, 'We were engaged. I suppose that's what you'd call it. Engaged. We lived together.'

'Here?'

The D.I. glanced at the tiny self-contained flatlet; at the divan bed, at the electric oven alongside the sink in one corner of the room, at the brightly-painted, second-hand chairs, the colour-washed walls, the gaudy mats, the gew-gaws which went to make up this miniature 'home'.

'We lived together,' repeated the young woman.

'The people at the college of technology hinted at it.' The D.I. moved his lips into a curve which was not quite

31

a smile. 'We're not shocked by such things. They're of no importance.'

'To us,' she murmured.

'Yes, of course. That's why we're here.' The D.I. glanced at his companion detective constable; the inevitable witness at such times, the invariable silent observer, with opened pocket-book and poised ballpoint. The D.I. continued, 'We'd have been here earlier, but – naturally – we wanted to locate his parents first. Next-of-kin. That sort of thing.'

'They're on holiday.'

'Yes. We know that now.'

'Touring.'

'Devon. Cornwall. We can't find anybody who knows exactly where. The A.A. are putting notices out, asking them to contact us.'

'And that's it, gentlemen. The situation, as it seems to be at this moment.' Gilliant paused long enough to examine the thirty-three pairs of eyes watching him. The thirty-three expressions, varying from open disgust through dead-pan to something not a million miles from compassion. Thirty-three high-rankers, each with a mind of his own. The thirty-three shoulders upon which rested the basic responsibility for the running of the whole M.P.D. He tried to read their collective mind, failed, then continued, 'We have to bear in mind that it *still* might be a hoax. It *might* be a coincidence. Personally, I don't think so, but it's something we can't ignore. It means we have to pursue two lines of enquiry. The one we're already pursuing. That the killing was done by somebody who knew the victim. Had a grudge. Shot him and that it just *happens* to coincide with the letter received by the *Tribune*. But, at the same time, we have to take the letter seriously. Assume that it *was* the writer of the letter who fired the shot. And take action along *those* lines, too.

'I'll ask for questions. Suggestions. Anything anybody might like to contribute to this discussion. But first of all I want Dr. Carr to have a few words with you.'

6.15 p.m.

The D.I. said, 'Somebody with a gun.'

'We don't know anybody with a gun.'

The tense – the plural pronoun – the phraseology of her answer to his implied question. Sudden death was no part of it. Murder was something which it refused to recognise. He was still alive, of course he was, he would at any moment open the door of this flatlet and join them in this rather ridiculous conversation.

The D.I. caught a sigh, suppressed it before it was fully born, leaned forward in his chair and, very gently, said, 'Miss Britten, he's dead.'

She nodded. It was a mere movement of the head; neither an acceptance nor a rejection. A nothing, and with no more meaning than the returned smile of a strange child.

'Miss Britten, he's dead,' repeated the D.I., sadly. 'He was shot. Murdered. And we have to find his killer.'

She intoned, 'We don't know anybody with a gun.'

'Somebody who didn't like him?' insisted the D.I. quietly.

'Everybody liked Steve. Why shouldn't they like him? He's nice. He's a nice person.'

The D.I. watched her face. That first sentence of her answer. A tentative acceptance of a frightening fact. The past tense, then the hurried cover-up, in the counter-question and the double remark. Like thick liquid dripping through filter-paper. Eventually, it would all come; the paper would become soggy, then tear, and the thick liquid of truth would spatterdash her brain and burn home the hateful hurt.

'Somebody killed him,' murmured the D.I. '*Somebody* didn't like him.'

Carr was one of a rare breed, a genuine expert who could enthuse. A Mortimer Wheeler, a Magnus Pyke, a Brian Horrocks. He could take a not-too-interested audience, not even notice their original apathy and, in a matter of minutes, have their eyes reflecting his own boundless enthusiasm.

That his expertise was allied to the horrific did nothing to quench his passion. Rape, murder, assault . . . these were the topics of his fanaticism. Not *as* rape, or murder, or assault, for he was a kindly man, with an impish sense of humour, but as endless and abstract problems; problems to be solved, via microscopes test-tubes, infra-red and ultra-violet rays and the whole battery of mystical paraphernalia at the disposal of the forensic scientist.

At this moment he was talking about ballistics and, as was his habit, he seemed to pin each fact to an invisible blackboard with a stab of his pipe stem.

He was saying, '. . . a .303, British, Mark Seven. Those of you with experience in Her Majesty's Forces will know what I mean. A common-or-garden "bullet". Solid. Pointed. Metal-covered. Manufactured by the million . . . still are.

'But not fired from any .303 rifle *we* can come up with. The groove-marks – the rifling-marks – don't tally. We're dealing with a very precise science, ballistics. A .303 requires a determined amount of spin – "twist", if you like – before it performs with maximum efficiency. It also requires a specific number of riflings, along the barrel of the weapon from which it's fired. Those riflings, and the amount of spin they give to the bullet as it travels along the barrel, determine its final range and accuracy.

'Don't misunderstand me, gentlemen. I'm not saying the weapon was inaccurate for present purposes. Nor am I suggesting that the range of the bullet wasn't sufficient, and more than sufficient, for those purposes. But they're *wrong*. .303, British, Mark Seven bullets are meant for long-range accuracy. Bisley stuff. And the weapon we're looking for isn't up to that sort of range or accuracy.

'We must assume, therefore, that the weapon has been either made, or adapted, to take this size of bullet. A home-made gun. A gun that's been altered. Something nobody can do with a do-it-yourself construction kit. And something very few people *can* do without running the risk of the gun exploding in their face when they pull the trigger.

'That's as much as I can tell you, gentlemen. That you're looking for a gun that isn't like an ordinary gun. It won't be recorded . . . at least, not as the sort of weapon it *is*. Common logic suggests that, if a man can adapt a gun to take a specific bullet, he can also make other alterations. A gun that will dismantle for easy and secret carriage. That's the first thing. Logic also suggests that the man – whoever he is – hasn't free access to ammunition. If he had he wouldn't go to the trouble of adapting the weapon for .303. He might do some work on it. It would be difficult, but not too difficult. Then he'd use the ammunition for which the gun was made. That's the sort of man you're after. The sort of gun you're after. Get me the gun and I'll match the bullet. Match the bullet with the gun and it's a step towards a conviction.'

'Questions. Observations. Suggestions.' Gilliant glanced around the faces staring back at him, from the body of the Recreation Room. He said, 'We have problems. We need solutions. Oh, and please smoke, if you wish.'

He sat down and waited.

Thirty-three senior police officers seemed to expel a communal sigh. A silent sigh which in fact was no sigh at all. Rather it was a relaxation of tightened emotions; a silent relief that now, at last, they knew the worst.

There was a shuffling of feet, a scraping of chairs, a clearing of throats, a fumbling for cigarettes, cheroots, pipes and pouches, followed by a ripple of tiny flames from matches and lighters. The air of the Recreation Room billowed with puffs and streamers of tobacco smoke.

Rucker broke the silence and Sullivan silently congratulated himself on guessing that Rucker *would* be the first to speak.

Rucker drawled, 'As from tomorrow, the rate-payers of this fair city will have a ball. At our expense, of course.'

'Easy, Rucker.'

The warning came from the man sitting immediately behind Rucker; from Sweetapple, the North End divisional chief superintendent and a man who, despite his name, was a known force to be reckoned with.

'Don't be so ridiculously "loyal", chief superintendent,' sneered Rucker. 'Testicles have been dropped on high. There's a stiff in the morgue, and . . .'

'*Rucker!*'

It even silenced Rucker. It was like a verbal volley-ball and it was hurled by Rucker's immediate chief, Sugden, assistant chief constable (crime) of the Lessford

36

Region of the M.P.D. The word seemed to send splinters ricochetting around the Recreation Room for a never-ending moment.

And never had Sullivan admired this burly colleague of his more. To rocket a senior police officer – a man holding the rank of detective chief superintendent – other than gently, and then in private, was almost unheard of. To do it before a roomful of his peers was something unique and something only a man like Sugden would even contemplate.

Sugden was from the old county constabulary area; one of a handful of pearls the sweeping together of the three forces had produced. He sought neither popularity nor admiration; he bobbied his own way – a way he himself would have happily described as 'rough as a bear's arse' – but, because of this don't-give-a-damn honesty, he *was* popular and he *was* admired and never ceased to wonder why. He was a man, perhaps the only man present, capable of curbing Rucker's excesses of contemptuous sarcasm; he could, and did, when necessary hammer Rucker into the ground by sheer weight of personality. Rucker hated him, and Sugden didn't give a toss, which made Rucker hate him even more.

Sugden growled, 'We will – *if* you don't mind, Chief Superintendent Rucker – concentrate upon essentials. We've all dropped goolies, in the past. Any man who says he hasn't is a bloody liar. I propose we don't waste time trying to pick 'em up. *Or* reminding each other of 'em. I propose we get our heads together and try not to drop any more.'

Gilliant smiled, and said, 'Thank you, Mr. Sugden. I second that proposal.'

The D.I. was making very little headway. He knew it, but he also knew the wall of disbelief had to be cracked before he and the detective constable could leave the tiny

37

flatlet. It was, he supposed, what the civil liberties crowd were always on about. One of their never-ending complaints. Harassment. Invasion of privacy. Police persecution, perhaps. They wrapped their niggling up in fancy language but, by Christ, they never had this size of nut to crack. They should try it sometime; they should sit where he was sitting; facing a young woman who was as near a zombie as didn't matter; who didn't answer questions, not because she didn't want to answer 'em, but because she didn't even *hear* the bloody things. And no, even that wasn't right, she heard them, but they didn't jell. One part of her mind had switched itself off. The rest was working perfectly, but there was a short-circuit somewhere; from the past, to the future, but with a by-pass which effectively ignored the present.

He tried again.

He said, 'Miss Britten. Who didn't like Steve?'

'Everybody likes Steve.' She looked shocked, genuinely amazed that anybody might think otherwise.

'Somebody disliked him.'

'No. He's a very popular . . .'

'*Somebody*.' The D.I. took a deep breath then, very carefully, said, 'He's dead, Miss Britten. He's dead because somebody shot him. Somebody shot him, therefore somebody disliked him.'

'No. You're wrong. Everybody likes Steve. Ask them. *Everybody* likes him.'

'Damn it, he's dead. DEAD.'

The D.I. shouted the last word directly into the face of the young woman. The detective constable looked worried. The D.I. closed his eyes for a moment and silently cursed himself for the sudden loss of control.

The young woman glanced at her wrist-watch, smiled and said, 'Look, he should be home soon. I'm making some coffee. Would you like a cup?'

*

Something about 'the fall of a sparrow'. The balance of the world tilts a little; things are never *quite* the same; the equilibrium of nature shifts slightly and has to be compensated.

If this, for a mere sparrow, what for a man? What for a young and healthy man – a popular man, with no real enemies – who, for no better reason than that he was walking along a certain pavement, at a certain moment of eternity, ceased? Ended? Became so much carrion?

And the parents of this carrion? The decent, run-of-the-mill Yorkshire folk, touring the southern counties and, at that moment, in Cornwall, gazing at the treasures of Cotehele House?

Richard Wrie scowled at the ancient cogs and wheels, then said, 'I don't get it. Why put a clock in a chapel in the first place?'

'There's lots o' clocks in chapels,' argued his wife Mabel.

'They don't chime. This one chimes,' insisted Wrie.

'How do *you* know?'

'It says so, here.' Wrie tapped his copy of the printed guide.

'Happen it's just been put there for us to see it better,' suggested his wife.

'Nay.' Wrie consulted the guide, once more. 'It says here, "in an unaltered state and in its original position". Damn, it hasn't even a face.'

'Richard!'

'Eh?'

'Remember where you are. Watch your language.'

'Oh, aye.' Wrie nodded solemn apology to the Almighty, then with typical northern phlegmatism added, 'It's not much good though, is it?'

'It's old.'

'Aye, well, happen so, but it wasn't much good when it

39

were made. No face. How can you tell t' time wi' a clock wi' no face?'

'It *chimed*, didn't it?'

'Aye. On the hour, that's what it says here.' He grinned, and said, 'By gum, they mun 'a been long sermons in them days.'

'Richard!'

They wandered round the chapel, admired the Flemish Triptych and the eighteenth-century Italian candlesticks, then left the chapel for the punch room.

'What's a punch room when it's at home?'

'I dunno. Shurrup, Richard, don't show your ignorance.'

'Nay, I'm damned . . .'

'Richard!'

'I like to know what I'm looking at, that's all.'

From the punch room to the white bedroom, from the white bedroom to the landings and from the landings to the red room.

'My word, Richard, just look at this bed.'

'Aye.'

'Innit lovely? All them red hangings. All them ribbons.'

'Bit mucky.'

'It's old, Richard. Seventeenth century. By gum, it's lovely, though.'

'Mucky, though.'

'Trust you to see no farther than muck.'

'And bloody 'ard, I'll bet.'

'Richard! Honest, sometimes I'm fair ashamed of you.'

'Aye, well. Gimme a spring-interior. That's all I'm saying.'

From the red room to the south room, from the south room to the old drawing-room, then on through Queen Anne's room and King Charles's room and from there out into the gardens once more.

Wrie breathed deeply and said, 'This is summat like. Good air down here, lass. Softer than it is up north.'

'It breeds soft folk.'

'I dunno. If they slept on them bloody beds . . .'

'But lovely flowers.'

'Aye. A nice show. I reckon they're two month earlier than us down here. At least two month.' He enjoyed another deep, chest-expanding breath, then said, 'What about t' mill, then?'

'It's a long walk,' she said dubiously.

'Aye.'

'But if you're interested.'

'Nay. I'll leave it to you. There's t' waterwheel, and t' forge.'

'I've seen waterwheels before now.'

'Aye.'

'And forges.'

'Well – y'know . . . I just thowt.'

'If you'd *like* to see 'em.'

'Nay. I'll leave it to you, lass.'

'I'm a bit tired,' she admitted, grudgingly.

'Aye. Me an' all.' As if to prove the point he stifled a gigantic yawn.

They wandered slowly towards the car park to where the uniformed constable was waiting, patiently, alongside the Austin Maxi.

The constable cleared his throat, and said, 'This your car, sir?'

'Aye.' Wrie's features took on that slightly aggressive look reserved for innocent motorists when approached by uniformed authority.

'Mr. Wrie? Mr. Richard Wrie?'

'Aye. What about it?'

And one more world began to tilt; the equilibrium of nature shifted slightly, and another sparrow fell.

Of themselves, and taken individually, the various details of that Friday evening were in no way peculiar. Nor were the personalities touched by the killing of Stephen Wrie headline-crackers; to a man, to a woman, they were ordinary people, angered or hurt, outraged or shocked but, other than that, each one the proverbial passenger on the Clapham omnibus; the 'reasonable man' and the 'reasonable woman'.

The man who had squeezed the trigger. . . .

The killer, the man the police had already dubbed 'John Doe', sipped what threatened to be an over-spill from his half-pint of beer before he placed the glass on the Formica-topped table and settled himself on the cushioned bench against the wall of the public bar.

He liked this pub. It was, he supposed, his 'local'; strictly speaking, not the nearest public house to his home, but the second-nearest and a place Mabel and he had visited on the few occasions when they'd sought quiet company, other than themselves.

Mabel. He'd been lucky in Mabel, he'd been lucky in Kim. A man could, perhaps, be too lucky in some things; use up all his luck in the choice of a wife, in the gift of an only child, and thereafter have no luck left for other things. Less important things perhaps, but in the long run things which also mattered.

Indeed his present circumstances were proof of this possible theory.

He was not a pauper; he would have been the first to admit that many people were far less affluent than himself. But, by God, what he had he'd worked for. He'd been no spendthrift, either in cash or in time; he'd invested wisely, and never once had he begrudged the hour upon hour of extra back-breaking work which had been necessary to drag the firm into a position of solvency. He lived in a house, long bought and paid for; a good house, standing in its own grounds, on the outskirts of Lessford. He'd been a good employer. Forget mock-modesty, he'd been a *good* employer, none better. He'd treated his work-people as a team, as fellow-craftsmen, whose pride in their skills placed them far above the petty squabblings of the nut-tighteners and spot-welders of the assembly lines. And they'd *been* that . . . until the damn union agitators had dropped poison into their ears. After that they'd been sheep. Lemmings. Every perfidious fool of 'em, hell-bent on self-destruction. They'd demanded impossible hours and impossible wages; impossible if a small firm was to survive in an industry which, from the start, was cut-throat.

And as far as possible he'd met those demands. As far as possible. But there was a limit, and when that limit had been reached he'd been blunt. He'd put his cards on the table, but the union lunatics had thought he was bluffing.

His very words were, 'Look, I'm sorry. We've lost a contract – a very important, government contract – and we've yet to find something to take its place. It's nobody's fault. It's just one of those things. But for the moment what you're asking is impossible. The firm's ticking over, little more than that. We're just about breaking even. If we get another contract – *when* we get another contract – when we've stabilised ourselves again, I'll consider these demands of yours. I'll consider them and, if possible, I'll meet them. But at the moment it can't be done.'

They'd thought he was bluffing. Maybe some men – some employers – did bluff in these things – did try to scare their own men with wild untruths. If so, it was a shameful thing. It condemned everybody. It ensured that the honest employers were disbelieved.

So there'd been wildcats and pickets, and lock-ins and

43

God knows what else. The trouble-makers had had their day. The bolshies had twisted disagreement until it had become open hatred.

Then one day he'd had enough.

He'd attended one of their meetings. Uninvited he climbed on to the platform at one of the local working men's clubs where the loudmouths had been holding out and, in less than two minutes, he'd silenced them and crushed them.

Again his very words, 'All right! You've heard what's been said. You've heard what's been advised. You've heard what you *should* do. Now I'll tell you what you *must* do. Look for work. Draw unemployment benefit. That's all you have left. The only choice left open to you. You can leave here, go home and tell that to your wife and kids. Every one of you. The firm doesn't exist any more. It's finished. It's closed. The doors and gates are locked. The machinery's been sold. Somebody else owns the bricks and mortar. Me? I've had enough. A gutful. And nobody – nobody on God's earth! – is going to jockey me into a position where the Official Receiver walks into *my* premises, and takes over. I'll not take that disgrace from any man. That's it, then. You're all out of a job. I'll leave you and wish you luck . . . and, by God, you're going to need it.'

For almost a fortnight they'd *still* thought it a massive bluff. Then the penny had dropped and, for a few days, he'd been almost a national hero. In the newspapers. On the radio. Even a couple of appearances on TV. 'The man who brought a union to its knees.'

The touch of a sardonic smile brushed his lips, at the memory.

Some hero! He's sliced off his own nose, to spite his face. He'd smashed men who had once been his friends. He'd destroyed a firm he'd given most of his life to create. *That* much of a hero; a hero with self-destructive principles . . . and the thousand times he'd wondered whether it had been worth it.

He was running. He didn't kid himself; he was running as far and as fast as he was able. He was running away from memories. Well, not memories. It was, he realised, impossible to run away from *memories*; a man carried his memories around with him; they stayed with him to the grave. Rather he was running away from *reminders*; the occasional meeting in the street of past employees he'd once respected; the house – the home – he'd built for his wife and child.

Perhaps, most of all, he was running away from bad-news headlines. Newspapers which emphasised the day-by-day crumbling of a nation. The United Kingdom. It was – it had become – a lousy, good-for-nothing country; a country top-heavy with bureaucracy, drowning in its own ocean of forms and returns and pettifogging applications, a country not fit to survive. A disgustingly apathetic country, led by men anxious to compromise with the wreckers.

There was a place. Moose Jaw, British Columbia. He'd never been there, but during the war one of his colleagues had talked much of Moose Jaw, British Columbia. And, accepting the home-sick exaggerations of a lonely Canuck, the place had sounded . . . It was difficult to explain, even to himself. It had sounded like England, as England *should* be; like a small town, with all the fierce pride which a small town *should* have.

Even the name. Moose Jaw. A fighting name; a name touched with wild history and present obstinacy. This thing he was doing; this killing of useless, weak-as-water Englishmen . . . in the final analysis, he supposed he was doing it in the name of Moose Jaw. To prove himself. To get the money and, at the same time, prove himself to be a worthy citizen for a town with a name like Moose Jaw.

He sipped his beer, and scowled as he contemplated the next move in this game of manhood.

Lennox.

If weight of newsprint meant anything, Lennox was the best-known copper in the whole of the Lessford Metropolitan Police District. He was a reporter's dream, a columnist's gift; his podgy finger had been in every forensic pie of any size for years; long before the creation of the M.P.D.; long before he'd graduated to the position of detective chief superintendent and Head of C.I.D. of the Bordfield Region; when he'd simply been Detective Superintendent 'Lenny' Lennox in the old Lessford City Police Force.

Lennox was a peg upon which to hang news and comment for a variety of reasons. In the first place he was not merely fat, he was obese; his figure (for want of a better name) consisted of a small sphere, atop a large sphere, with bulky and ridiculously short appendages which went under the names of arms and legs; and, as so often happens with such men, his joviality was such that his shape, plus his manner, reminded everybody of those long-dead music-hall comedians : those red-nosed, baggy-trousered, small-hatted, stand-up comics who once upon a time had waddled out in front of some outlandish backdrop and virtually hurled a non-stop gag routine at a delighted audience. Lennox was the elderly Billy Bunter of the police world; a forensic Falstaff who wheezed and roared a bewilderingly eccentric path through even the most solemn of crime enquiries.

Add to this the fact that he dressed the part. His forte was gaudy bow-ties and dazzlingly brilliant pullovers; outdated suits and ridiculous headgear. He was a blatant and unashamed eccentric, in a profession renowned for grey uniformity.

To be laughed at, to be chuckled over, to be guffawed about, but not by those scores of would-be clever Johnnies who had learned, too late, that those layers of fat covered a volpine mind, capable of outwitting the best of 'em, plus a dogged patience of which an American Indian might be proud.

At the moment he was asleep in the wide, spring-broken armchair at his home near Lessford boundary. He was (as he would have put it) zizzing; his turn for take-over of the enquiry started at midnight, at which time he relieved his immediate boss, Harris, the assistant chief constable (crime) for the Bordfield Region. Meanwhile, he snoozed and snored.

Harris was not sleeping. Having launched the creation of a full-scale Operations Centre in the Recreation Room, he'd left the headquarters building and was now in Kingsley's office of *The Lessford and Bordfield Tribune,* examining a pull of tomorrow's front page, complete with its black-lined, front-page editorial.

The editorial was head-lined . . .

THE APOLOGY WHICH IS TWENTY-FOUR HOURS TOO LATE

It read:

This newspaper is not unique. Like every other news-paper in the United Kingdom, it has made mistakes. Unlike some newspapers it has, where necessary, ad-mitted those mistakes. More than once it has apolo-gised to people whom it might have, unknowingly, injured or offended.

An apology is again called for, but this time it is an apology which, alas, will do no good. It will neither

47

ease a hurt, nor comfort those deserving of sympathy.

Nevertheless, it is made with no small shame and in the knowledge that it is far too late.

The following letter was received at this office on the morning of Thursday, July 28th.

There followed a photographic reproduction of the letter, signed by 'J.D.'.

The editorial ended . . .

The nature of a newspaper is such that a steady flow of similar letters are delivered to its offices. The vast bulk are written by unfortunate men and women who crave publicity or who nurse some imagined grudge against society.

Because familiarity does indeed breed contempt, these letters are ignored. Not merely by us, but by every newspaper in the United Kingdom. That they should not be ignored has been proved by the death yesterday of Stephen Wrie. Wrie, a student of Lessford College of Technology, was gunned down in King Street, Lessford, at thirty minutes past midday yesterday. He was killed by an unknown assassin and for no apparent reason. Pending proof to the contrary, we of this newspaper must accept responsibility for his death. We did not insert the small ad., as instructed by the unknown writer of the above letter. We must therefore assume that Wrie's death is a direct result of our failure to do so.

This then is an unreserved, but we realise quite useless, apology. We publish it with the humble assurance, to all our readers, that we have learned our lesson.

'Neat.' Harris dropped the pull on to Kingsley's desk. 'It tells the truth, but doesn't drop the police. We're in the clear, officially.'

'I don't want anybody else killed.' Kingsley's voice was

that of a tired and defeated man. He said, 'I think I should resign. I haven't yet made up my mind, but I rather think I should.'

'A gesture,' growled Harris, impatiently.

'A necessary gesture.' Kingsley fingered the pull nervously. 'I doubt if any editor – any newspaper – has printed a more sincere apology.' He looked at Harris, and added, 'Bear – your deputy chief constable – helped with the draft.'

'Cunning.'

'I don't want anybody else killed,' repeated Kingsley.

'Mmm.' Harris compressed his lips at what he saw as a weak man. He said, 'He'll be at you again, of course.'

'Who?'

' "J.D.". John Doe. What the hell he calls himself.'

'I – I don't see why he should.'

'He reads the paper. Presumably. That last bit, about "humble assurance" and the "learned our lesson" bit. It's for *his* benefit.'

'Bear didn't . . .'

'It's a come-on.' The professional man-hunter smiled appreciation of a beautifully constructed ploy. ' "Our readers" – meaning *him*. Neat.'

'Look, we want no part . . .'

' "We"?'

'This newspaper.'

'You personally?'

'No. This newspaper. We don't want . . .'

'You don't want him caught?'

'No. I didn't say that. Of course I want him caught.'

'That's the trap.' Harris tapped the pull with a forefinger. 'Don't arse it up, Kingsley. The next killing *will* be on your conscience.'

'You've taken some finding, Snide.'

'Look, I dunno wot . . .'

'All that "Williams" crap on the side o' your cart.'

'You've no bleedin' right to . . .'

'And all the time it's you.' The elderly copper shook his head slowly, sadly and with solemn disapproval. 'You've taken some finding. You've wasted a lot o' valuable time.'

The elderly copper and the young detective sergeant were still working in double-harness. They were 'following leads'. They'd been 'following leads' for more than six hours; asking questions, noting mentioned names, finding the owners of those names, then asking more questions and noting other mentioned names. As a game it left Silly Buggers at the start-line. It was almost as daft, as non-productive, as House-to-House Enquiries. But it filled notebooks with names and addresses and, when those names and addresses were transferred to the Murder File, the picture produced was one of· wild activity, which was all the H.M. Inspector of Constabularies asked for at his annual wander through the annals of the force.

The elderly copper was happy to oblige. The young detective sergeant was content to tag along and learn.

And now they were in North End; that part of Lessford (that part of *every* city) which breaks the hearts of men of goodwill. It had once been an area of back-to-back slum dwellings. It was now an area of high-rise slum dwellings. Only the dimension had altered; where it had once been horizontal, it was now perpendicular; the layers of muck had been carefully bulldozed into cubic heaps.

Henry Carlton 'Snide' Rubens had been born among the muck, received an education in the various arts of law-breaking among the muck, and still lived there among the muck, a learned professor (at the very least, the holder of a doctorate) within the sphere of fiddles, small-time crookedness and general shady dealings. A man of some stature within his own community. A man of nc stature at all within the community of law-enforcement.

He said, 'You've no bleedin' right to . . .'

'And all the time it's you. You've taken some finding. You've wasted a lot o' valuable time.'

'Wot the bleedin' 'ell . . . ?'

' "Williams", it says, on the side o' your handcart.'

'An' wot if it does? I ain't . . .'

'You know me, Snide.'

'Too bloody right, I know you. You're the . . .'

'It's illegal.'

'Worris?'

'Humping a handcart around the streets with some-body else's name painted on the side.'

'Don't be so bloody barmy. 'Ow the 'ell can it be . . . ?'

'Snide.' The elderly copper poked Rubens in the stomach – plumb centre on the solar plexus – with a finger as stiff as a poker. 'Don't use naughty language, lad. And don't argue so much.' The stiffened finger jabbed home again, Rubens gasped a little and doubled forward slightly. 'If I say it's illegal, it's illegal. I don't bluff, lad. There's a reason for these things.'

'Wot things?'

'Having the proper name painted on your handcart. It makes sure hard-working coppers aren't led up gum trees.'

'You knew where I was. You knew I . . .'

'About half past twelve,' interrupted the elderly copper.

'Eh?'

'King Street.'

'Worrabout King Street?'

'A young lad was shot.'

'Oh, *that*.'

'You know about it?'

51

'I've 'eard.'

'Who told you?'

'I dunno. Some bloke I . . .'

'Did you need telling?'

'You what?'

'Telling? Did you need telling?'

'I'm not bloody psychic. 'Ow the 'ell . . . ?'

'You were there, lad.'

'Eh?'

'In King Street. With that handcart o' yours.'

'When?'

'When the lad was shot.'

'Who says?'

'*I* say. *We* say. Me and this colleague o' mine. And a lot o' other people say.'

'Oh!'

'And we don't yet know who shot him. It could have been you, Snide. It could very easily have been you.'

'Jesus, Joseph and Mary!'

'Take your time, lad.'

'You *what*?'

'No rush. We've found you after a deal o' looking. We can wait.'

'Wait? Wot the 'ell for?'

'You tell us. We're asking 'em. You're answering 'em.'

In technical parlance this was known as 'putting on the frighteners' or, occasionally, as 'hitting him where it'll raise his voice a few octaves'. The ins and outs of such law-enforcement basics were not to be found within the covers of *Moriarty's Police Procedure and Administration*, nor were they included within the curriculum of any Police Training College but, as with anabolic steroids, they were necessary to keep ahead of the field.

Not for the moment – not for one split second – did the elderly copper suspect Snide of murder. Murder was way and gone to hell out of Snide's league. But Snide was a consistent law-bender and as such a perpetual nuisance; he wasted far too many man-hours by committing pint-sized crimes. It was therefore necessary to discourage Snide's naughty tendencies as much and as often as possible. To let him *know* that he could be pin-pointed in King Street, at a specific time, if such pin-pointing became necessary; that the name 'Williams' painted on the sides of his handcart would no longer fool anybody; that the con of being an honest, hard-working window-cleaner had run its course.

And, for good measure, make him sweat marbles for a few minutes, wretched in the belief that he was a suspect in a murder enquiry.

There was also (as the elderly copper knew) a spin-off to this uncharitable attitude to petty crooks.

The sprats of the criminal pond deplore the crime of murder. Not because they are overflowing with brotherly love. Not because they hold human life in any way sacred. Not because they subscribe to a belief in non-violence. They dislike murder because murder is a damn nuisance to them. For purely selfish reasons they have an aversion to criminal homicide. It brings the cops out; lots and lots of cops. And every cop starts asking questions; lots and lots of questions. The accumulative effect brings on the screaming shudders.

The elderly copper knew these simple facts of criminal life. He knew that throughout Lessford, throughout Bordfield, throughout the whole M.P.D. area dozens of world-weary policemen – constables, sergeants, C.I.D., uniformed branch – would be putting the frighteners on dozens and scores of tiny, insignificant germs like Snide. And maybe one of those tiny, insignificant germs would drop a hint, name a name, panic and say something he shouldn't say in the holy cause of self-preservation.

Some very nasty crimes had been cleared up by hitting a comparatively innocent little tea-leaf where it would raise his voice a few octaves.

The Austin Maxi entered the southern entrance to the Blackwall Tunnel at a steady sixty. Its speed and its no-nonsense barging from lane to lane until it claimed the traffic stream it required caused even the militant motorists of the metropolis to raise their brows in amazement.

Mabel Wrie said, 'Careful, Richard. Getting *us* killed won't help.'

There was no answer, nor did she expect one. She knew this husband of hers; this blunt-spoken, pig-headed Yorkshireman; this man without frills, whose code of life was as harsh and as immovable as the outcrops of his beloved Pennines. A man slow to anger, but whose anger when roused knew no bounds. A man equally sparing with his love. Slow to anger, slow to love, but when he gave he gave without qualification and forever.

To him the loss of an only child was like the loss of a limb. As painful and as disabling as that. The ruination of his future. The obliteration of his own reason for living.

And the *murder* of that only child . . .

She glanced at the stone-set face, at the hard dry eyes, at the turned-down corners of the tightly-closed lips. At the countenance of naked vengeance.

And although she knew this husband of hers, for the first time in her life she was frightened.

'They called him Steve,' murmured Sullivan. 'Stephen. And his father's name's Richard. It seems to bring it home a bit. More than usual.'

'More coffee?' asked Mary Sullivan.

'Thanks.' Sullivan pushed his cup an inch or so across the table.

Sullivan. Richard Sullivan, life-time copper, lauded and applauded by his fellows as one of the finest police-men ever to take the oath; deputy chief constable of Less-ford Metropolitan Police District. But at the moment Dick Sullivan, husband and father.

Sullivan's house was a very nice house. Few coppers (even deputy chief constables) can afford an architec-turally-planned abode, with bedrooms of a chosen size and shape, with dining room, lounge and study meticu-lously placed and windowed to catch the maximum of sunlight, with a kitchen on a par with the adverts in the Sunday supplements, with two beautiful bathrooms and two comfortable bogs. At the present going-price Sulli-van's house, and its surrounding acre or so of land, would have made one hell of a hole in thirty thousand quid, and common-or-garden coppers (even common-or-garden deputy chief constables) do not handle loot of that nature.

Fortunately Sullivan had a son, and Sullivan's son was almost a trained architect; he was on the last lap prior to being pronounced a young man fit and capable of designing the various topographical flim-flam which go to make up a modern city. Sullivan had bought the land. His son, Steve, had designed the house. The combination of copper and up-and-coming architect had ensured that the cost of the materials had been little more than ware-house price and Sullivan, Steve and a handful of Steve's cronies in the building trade had done the actual muscle-work.

The result was virtually a show house in the village of Upper Drayson in the old county constabulary area. Sullivan's retirement house, in fact.

And now Sullivan was sitting in his posh kitchen, drinking mid-evening coffee with his wife, Mary, and ruminating upon the side-issues of the King Street killing.

'It could,' said Sullivan, sombrely, 'have been *our* Steve.'

'Heaven forbid!'

'Amen to that,' Sullivan sighed. 'But it *could* have, Mary. Dammit, the lad was just walking along a pavement. He just happened to be *there*.'

'And the *Tribune* knew?'

'They knew, they didn't know. Don't blame the *Tribune*. A letter like that. Who the hell takes it seriously?'

Sullivan spooned brown sugar into the coffee. It was almost an absent-minded movement, as if his thoughts were miles away in the past, in the future or, if in the present, not within the walls of the kitchen.

'Bobbying's changed,' he said, heavily.

'Bobbying?'

'It's different. It hasn't the fun. The gusto.'

'I can't remember you ever thinking murder was funny.'

'No, that's the wrong word.' Sullivan finished stirring the coffee and placed the spoon in the saucer. This movement too had the air of absent-mindedness about it, it was a little slow and without even the slight concentration usually accorded it. 'Not fun. But enjoyment. Damn it, not even enjoyment. What word am I looking for?'

'Excitement?' suggested Mary Sullivan.

'Aye.' He nodded. 'That could be the word. The excitement it once had. But, I dunno.' He stared at his cup with a saddened expression. 'These days – nothing. No sparkle. No zip. The job's changed out of all recognition.'

He sipped at his coffee and again the inattention was there, the lack of mindfulness. Like a musical box whose lid has been left open too long, whose tinkling tune is slowing down and on the point of giving out its last few notes. The analogy prompted her own analogy.

She said. 'A little like the musical director of a big orchestra.'

'Eh?' He blinked and concentrated his attention.

'You,' she smiled.

'I don't know what you're talking about.'

'You were once the conductor,' she said. 'Before that you were the lead violinist. And before that one of the players. Now all you can do is listen and hope nobody plays too many false notes.'

'Ah!' He grinned a little self-consciously as the gist of her words became clear. He murmured, 'A bit past it.'

'Not necessarily.'

'The same thing.'

She was suddenly very serious. She said, 'I think you remember North End too often.'

'Great days.' He smiled and for a moment his eyes went out of focus.

'You thought so. I wasn't too sure.'

'Oh, come on, pet. They were *great* days.'

'I wonder if Mrs. Sweetapple thinks so?'

'Sweetapple's enjoying himself.' There was enthusiasm tinged with regret in his tone. 'Old Sweetapple's the sort. He'll be in there sorting 'em out.'

'Dick! Dick!' It was a plea. Almost a cry of despair. 'He's like you, like you once were. Conducting the orchestra. Having a whale of a time. She'll be at home, worrying.'

'Oh!' He stared at her face, concerned, then asked, 'Did *you* worry? Y'know, really *worry*?'

'With you waging war against those animals. Every day. What do *you* think?'

'It's being a copper,' he said, simply. 'What bobbying's really about. And being a copper's wife.'

'I know.'

'When we got married. You knew what I was. You knew I . . .'

57

'I'm not complaining. It's you who's doing the complaining.'

'Me?' Again she'd lost him. His expression was one of non-understanding.

'Let's assume.' She took a cigarette from a packet on the table and lit it as she talked. 'Let's assume Chief Superintendent Sweetapple left. Went to another force. Anything. The chief superintendentship became vacant. They wouldn't but let's assume, let's assume they offered *you* it. Ignore the drop in pay. The drop in rank. All the externals. Assume they made the offer. Would you accept?'

'That's a hell of a . . .'

'Would you accept?' She allowed the repeated question to ride on cigarette smoke.

He screwed his mouth around, then chewed at his lower lip, then raised his eyebrows, then lowered them. All the facial contortions supposedly connected with the making of a great decision.

Then he sighed and said, 'I'd think about it.'

'Which means you would.'

'Aye, I reckon so.'

'And it's *me* who's complaining?' she said, softly.

'I don't see what . . .'

'You hate the job,' she said, patiently. 'The job you now have, not the job you once had. Not policing. But being the musical director. Making the decisions. Sitting in an office. Not – what is it? – not "feeling collars". You want to be out front there. On the streets. In there sorting 'em out. Like Sweetapple. *That's* policing. What you're doing isn't, not by your yardstick.'

'Somebody has to do it,' he muttered.

'What?'

'All the paperwork. All the forms. All the high-level chinwag. *Somebody* has to do it.'

'But not you.'

The three words had layers of meaning. They were like a multi-deck sandwich and the contents of that sandwich, the various decks, included concern, sympathy, exasperation, mild annoyance and strained affection. In all their life Mary Sullivan had never uttered three words which had contained as much significance.

She drew on her cigarette and waited.

Sullivan took a deep breath, then said, 'As deputy chief constable I've no option but to . . .'

'As deputy chief constable.'

'It's what I am,' he said in a low voice.

'What you are. But not what you're enjoying.'

'Dammit, it's promotion. Promotion with the lid off. I never expected to get anywhere as . . .'

'You'd have been retired,' she reminded him.

'Maybe,' he conceded.

'Damn! You know perfectly well you would.' The annoyance lost some of its mildness. 'Collins has retired. Raff . . .'

'Raff had no option. His nerve went.'

'Ripley . . .'

'Ripley shot himself,' he said, savagely. 'Bloody hell, woman.'

'Don't swear at me. You're not a deputy chief constable in *this* house.' Suddenly their mutual love jack-knifed and seemed to become mutual hatred. Their voices hardened. Their eyes glinted. They faced each other across the table and each sought words with which to hurt the other. She snapped, 'And don't tell me about Charlie Ripley. He was too much like you for me not to know exactly what *he* was like.'

'What the devil's that supposed to mean?'

'Pig-headed.'

'Is that what I am?'

'Do you need telling?'

'And this place? This house? Is that all it means? That I'm . . .'

'What do you know about this house? You're never here.'

'I'm here now.'

'Well, thank *you*.'

'For Christ's sake . . .'

'I will tell you, Richard Sullivan.' She stabbed the air in his direction with the two fingers holding the cigarette. 'You are here, when you can spare time from that infernal office of yours. When, for an odd hour or so, you can convince yourself that your precious police force can tick over without your personal supervision. *That's* when you're here. *That's* when I see you. When Steve sees you.'

'Steve? He's out somewhere. I'm here at home and he's off gallivanting.'

'Should he wait? Should he sit around, waiting for the arrival of his lord and master? Hasn't he a life of his own? Is *that* what you want?'

'Mary, for God's sake . . .'

'No!' Her eyes blazed and what had been pent up for months, for years, came out with a rush. 'That's you, Richard. It's what you've become. Authority. The man who cracks the whip. But the man who can't delegate authority. Who thinks nobody can do it – anything – unless he's there standing over them. And you like it. You *love* it.'

'What the hell . . . ?'

'What is it? Three months from now? You'll be doing press-ups. Running-on-the-spot. Deep-breathing exercises. God knows what else. Making a complete fool of yourself, because the annual medical will be coming up. And you'll have to be fit. Oh, yes, you'll have to be fit for one more year of your precious authority.'

'Look. If you think that . . .'

'Think it? I *know* it. Steve knows it. Everybody knows it. You should have retired three years ago, at least three years ago. Since then you've been holding on by the skin of your teeth. Year at a time. Medical at a time. You're an old man, Richard. Not ancient. Not doddering. But for policing *you're an old man*. For God's sake face up to it.'

She stopped. She was flush-faced and trembling slightly. She smoked the cigarette fitfully; lifting it to her lips, then lowering it and blowing the smoke out before inhaling it. She thought she'd gone too far and the thought frightened her a little. Had she over-stated her case? Had she wounded this proud husband of hers, really wounded him, not merely angered him – that wasn't important, they'd had their full quota of married rows – but this time really *hurt* him?

In a gentler voice she said, 'Dick, you've seen it yourself. Scores of times. You've told me. You've blamed them every time. The older men. The superintendents, the inspectors, yes, even the chief constables. Hanging on. Log-jamming the promotion ladder. A sergeant stops one man. An inspector stops two. I've heard you. You've had it all worked out. Now, how many promotions does a deputy chief constable stop? I won't tell you. You can work it out for yourself.' She leaned forward and closed the fingers of her free hand over his forearm. She almost whispered, 'Darling, I don't want them saying it about you. That – that you're in the way. Past your best, but in the way. You're not – I'm sorry, I didn't mean to suggest that you were – but if you stay on. Please. Think about it. Just think about it.'

Night . . .

The killer (John Doe) lay on his back, locked the fingers
of his hands at the nape of his neck and stared into the
darkness of the bedroom. The nightly ritual. The bring-
ing forth of memories. The deliberate self-torture.

The bed, for example. He could spread-eagle his legs
beneath the covers, the whole of the double-bed was now
his territory. She wasn't there any more to claim her share,
to cling to the bedclothes when he turned and threatened
to drag them from her. She wasn't warm and soft against
his back. She didn't sleep with her mouth slightly open
making tiny snoring noises. She didn't awaken him in the
small hours when she climbed from bed to visit the bath-
room. Even things like that . . . even *those* things were
things he missed.

But he hadn't shamed her.

Thank God for that, she hadn't lived long enough for
him to shame her.

'It's all right, dear. Don't worry. A little setback. All
firms suffer setbacks occasionally. It's proof that we're
starting to *matter*.'

And at that very moment the firm had been twitching
in its first death-throes.

'Darling, you mustn't believe idle gossip. You really
mustn't. Get well. Then come down and see for yourself.
We're holding our own. More than holding our own.'

And even *he* couldn't get into the damn factory on
that day. The purblind fools had staged a 'lock-in'. Or
was it a 'sit-in'? Some bloody idiotic phraseology their
chosen masters had come up with. It hadn't mattered
what the name was. 'Finis'. 'The End'. 'Curtain'. They
all meant the same.

Three days later she'd died. He liked to think she'd

never known, that she might have had certain suspicions but she'd never really *known*.

He had, he supposed, gone a little mad. A little crazy with combined hurt. It was possible, more than possible. If so it explained a lot of things. His hour of glory, for example, when he'd stormed into the clubroom and made the speech millions had wanted somebody to make.

'. . . And nobody – nobody on God's earth ! – is going to jockey me into a position where the Official Receiver walks into *my* premises, and takes over. I'll not take that disgrace from any man . . .'

Mabel, my pet. Mabel, my sweet. I really meant it when I said it. Truly. I really meant it. But the Inland Revenue and the Customs and Excise and the dozen or so suppliers of raw materials. And finally the bank. I really didn't know how much I owed. This, that, the other. And even you, my pet. I'm not blaming you – God knows, I'm not criticising you – but even *you.* Everything in our joint names. And that meant death duty.

Oh God, Mabel, darling Mabel, why did you have to die? *Why did you have to die?*

'My son,' said Richard Wrie. 'I wanna see him.'

There was an unnatural breathless quality about his voice. A brittle harshness. Almost a panting. As if the words had had to fight their way out past his throat.

The detective constable said, 'It's late, sir. It's past midnight. Tomorrow morning, perhaps.'

Wrie stared unbelievingly. The truth was he *didn't* believe, it was beyond his comprehension, well beyond his comprehension. Damnation, he was talking about his son. His only son, for God's sake. Not some stranger. Not some passing acquaintance. Not some distant member of his somewhat sprawling family. *His son!* In effect, what had once been his future and what now no longer existed.

63

Nor, in fairness, was the detective constable being un-reasonable. At least not by his own yardstick. He under-stood, or thought he understood, this man's loss. He understood this man's misery. But the man was tired, he'd just completed a long car journey – one hell of a long car journey – and he was dog-tired. He looked dog-tired, a mix of black-and-grey stubble shadowed his jowls and cheeks, his eyes were red-rimmed and dulled with weariness. Moreover he was an old man. He wasn't up to long-distance driving and, if the time of the message from the Cornish police was anything to go by, very fast long-distance driving. This old lad must have had his foot down every inch of the way. What he needed now was bed, and for as long as possible.

The detective constable said, 'Go to bed, Mr. Wrie. Leave it to us. We'll do all that's necessary.'

'Don't be a bloody fool!'

'Now look . . .'

'I wanna see my lad.'

He was unfortunately a very young detective con-stable. Young in years, young in experience, young in the ways of handling bereavement. He was also very conscious of his C.I.D. status. A mite officious and, because this was his first murder enquiry, anxious to make a name for himself.

His face and voice hardened a little.

He said, 'Don't call me a fool, Mr. Wrie. I'm prepared to make allowances, but there are limits. Now get off back home and we'll contact you when we need you to . . .'

That was when Wrie hit him.

It was a full-blooded, ball-fisted smash and it missed the point of the jaw by a mere fraction. The blow was accompanied by a sob of sheer frustration and it carried all the weight of pent-up emotion with which Wrie had been saddled since hearing the news of his son's death.

It sprawled the D.C. on to the polished floor of the Lessford D.H.Q. entrance hall and skidded him on his back, until his skull smacked against the wood of the public counter. For a moment Wrie looked as if he might follow through and continue with his feet. But instead he drew in a deep, shuddering breath and stood there, arms and head hanging low, while a uniformed constable vaulted the counter and grabbed him in a neck-lock.

The P.C. said, 'Easy! Easy, Mr. Wrie. Just cool off . . . eh?'

'Lemme go.' Wrie seemed drained of all emotion. He offered no resistance to the constable's hold. He muttered, 'I shouldn't. I'm sorry. Lemme go.'

The constable released his hold and Wrie stood there and watched the detective constable haul himself upright. The D.C. wiped a trickle of blood from the corner of his mouth with the back of his hand, then fingered the already-swelling side of his jaw.

He gasped, 'Inside.'

It was little more than a whisper, but high-pitched and quavering with something not too far removed from hysterical rage.

'Mick.' The word was a warning. The uniformed constable was aghast at this sudden turn of events. He said, 'Cool it, Mick. You don't want to . . .'

'Inside.' The D.C. leaned against the counter, still groggy and with eyes blazing uncontrolled fury. He snarled, 'You're a witness, Barrett. Assault on Police. The old bastard *hit* me. Christ knows why, but . . .'

'Aye.' Wrie raised his head and some semblance of life returned to his expression. He said, 'Keep yon bugger away from me, 'else I'll fell him.'

'No, you won't, Mr. Wrie. You've too much gumption.'

Lennox descended the last step of the stairs leading from the first floor and the Operations-Centre-cum-Recreation-Room, having been hurriedly buzzed by a worried desk sergeant. He waddled across the entrance foyer and, without actually smiling, gave an impression of sympathetic but unconditional welcome.

The D.C. gasped, 'Sir, he . . .'

'Shurrup.' Lennox didn't even look at the still-dazed D.C.

'He *hit* me.'

'You fell.' Without pausing in his progress across the entrance hall Lennox added, 'That right, constable?'

'Er – yes, sir,' agreed the uniformed constable.

'You fell. Away and get yourself patched up.' Lennox reached Wrie, placed banana-thick fingers on the older man's arm and said, 'Now then, old son. We've been waiting for you. It's good of you not to have wasted any time.'

Lennox and Wrie ignored the speechless detective constable.

The desk sergeant who had telephoned for Lennox leaned over the counter, touched the D.C. on the shoulder and in a low voice said, 'Son . . . tha knows. Tha's tripped up. If I were thee I'd go off duty. Get thi' sen' patched up. Start a new day in t' morning. Tha'll feel better for it.'

And in a cell at Her Majesty's Prison, Leeds – in one of the human pigeon-holes which went to make up the complex which the locals knew as 'Armley' – a man turned on his comfortless bed and slept fitfully.

He was there because he had done what in effect Wrie had done. He had hit a police officer. Harder, more savagely and with a pick-handle, but the only difference was one of degree.

And of course motive.

Clarke had seen the firm go down the Swanee, watched it being strangled out of existence by foxes leading sheep. He'd fought. He'd fought like the very devil alongside the old man, and not just because he'd married the old man's daughter. He'd fought because the old man had been right, so bloody *right*! Between them, just the two of them, they'd smashed a way through the picket lines. Not once. A dozen times. More. And for what? As a token gesture, no more than that. Because two men couldn't run a whole damn factory. No matter how hard they worked, no matter how they schemed to divide the work-load, it couldn't be done.

They'd been licked. Licked by fools. And Clarke didn't take kindly to being licked by fools.

The old man had had his own troubles. Not just the firm. His wife, too, a wife who was dying and from whom the truth had to be hidden.

But Clarke . . . Clarke had been a free agent.

He'd heard rumours and attended meetings. Secret meetings, meetings at which firm-jawed men had stood at a table draped with the Union Jack and preached a form of counter-revolution. The words 'New Fascist Party' had been whispered and, by Christ, good men had had cause enough to be angry. And he'd liked what he'd heard; he'd agreed with it and wanted part of it. So he'd joined men of his own persuasion when they'd organised a protest group to heckle some left-wing militant.

Just to heckle. That's why he'd gone along. To heckle and shout the man down. But the bully-boys of the left had had their own ideas and within minutes the rough-house had been like all hell let loose. The bolshie bastards had had weapons; knives, knuckle-dusters, clubs. God knows what else. And when the cops had streamed in Clarke had just managed to twist a pick-handle from one of the reds and was heading for the thick of things. And why not? These pseudo-political destructors had smashed the old man, had taken a damn good firm with damn

67

good conditions and damn good wages and systematically ruined it. Fixed it. Hammered it out of existence.

And – okay – he'd gone berserk. A little berserk. To repay some of the hurt. That's all. To show *them* what it was like to be smashed.

Then the cops . . .

Jesus wept, they'd been on *their* side! Some bullshit about the meeting being legal. Approved. Democratically allowed. And the cops had been on *their* side. The cops! Part of the so-called 'Establishment'. And on the side of *those* bloody animals.

That had put the tin hat on things.

Except that the copper hadn't been wearing a tin hat. Not even a helmet; somebody had knocked his helmet for a burton long before he made a charge to grab Clarke. And Clarke had hit out. And the copper had ended up in a hospital bed with a dozen or so stitches in his skull. And Clarke hadn't given a damn; what the hell was the use when even the *cops* were on their side?

He'd earned himself six months and lucky to get off as lightly as that. The stipendiary magistrate had told him he was lucky. Had told him he was lucky and, in as many words, had said that his luck was based upon two things. He'd never been through police hands before. And he'd been scrapping on the right side; legally the wrong side but morally the right side. That's what the magistrate had said in as many words.

But six months was still six months, okay four months with good behaviour. Four months away from Kim. Four months cooped up with petty tearaways, with thieves and housebreakers, with perverts and pimps, with the scum of humanity.

In 'Armley'.

And Clarke turned on his comfortless bed, slept fitfully, but was unaware that his hero, his father-in-law, was already a killer and far more of a criminal than he would ever be.

Nor was Preston sleeping well.

Preston the loud-mouth. Preston the very epitome of the red-necked cop. Preston the lout, the bish-bash-bosh wallah, the original bull running wild in the forensic china-shop.

Ah yes, but men make noise for a variety of reasons.

With Preston it was a cover-up; a thick, near-impenetrable layer of noise, beneath which simmered frustrations and incompetences.

One of the frustrations lay asleep in the bed alongside him.

Preston's wife was beautiful. Only a raving blind man would have disputed that self-evident fact. Beautiful: not merely 'good-looking' or 'nice' or any of the other adjectives which go to make up the various levels of less-than-perfect. She was *beautiful*, period. She walked down the street and men gawped a little; they mentally stripped her and many ravished her in their sudden imagination. It was that brand of beauty: tawny, vibrant and seemingly alive with subdued passion. She was ten years younger than Preston and those who knew them tended to wonder at what she'd seen in him or, conversely, how the hell a man like Preston had netted such a gem.

Some gem!

Beauty, so the saying goes, is only skin-deep and the wise guy who thought that one out had Preston's wife in mind. Inside that red-hot skin she was all ice. All ambition. All cold, calculating go-getting.

Preston could literally pin-point his progression up the ladder of promotion; each rung had been celebrated by a few weeks of wild excess; fornication gone mad, but with a very controlled madness.

Then had come the tapering off. The 'Not tonight, I'm

69

tired' period. Then not even that. The contemptuous turning away, with neither excuse nor apology. The silent but mutually understood arrangement; that Preston was one man who had to *earn* his so-called 'conjugal rights'.

Oh, there'd been occasions. Odd times. When he'd felt a particularly important collar. When *she'd* had the 'urge'. Promises, reminders of what was in store, come the next peg up the pole.

But since Rucker, since Rucker had leap-frogged him and grabbed the chair *he'd* hoped to occupy. Since then not so much as a quick sniff. Nothing!

He'd begged a few times. Imagine that . . . Detective Superintendent Preston pleading for a quick romp. And with his own wife. With the bitch who gave every outward appearance of having everlasting ants in her cute little panties.

Her and Rucker between them. Two right bloody animals, each trying to twist the knife just that little bit deeper. Each watching him squirm. Each smiling. Each having one hell of a time at his expense.

Nice going, Preston. That you can sleep at all is something of a marvel. That you shout and bawl isn't to be wondered at. If that blanket of noise ever became threadbare, you'd weep.

That or die of shame.

'It is,' said Lennox, solemnly, 'part of the law. Your son, I know. But for the moment, pending the inquest, he belongs to the coroner.'

'Nay. He's my lad, mister. Law nor nowt else can alter that.'

'True.' Solemnity, mixed with genuine solicitude, sat awkwardly on Lennox's podgy, music-hall face. He pushed his hands deeper into the pockets of his shapeless trousers and said, 'The law's an idiot, old son. It ain't

70

geared for situations like this. Trouble is, it's still the law
. . . see?'

'I dunno what his mam'll say,' muttered Wrie.

'Where is she?' asked Lennox.

'Wi' her sister. At her sister's place. I thowt . . . tha
knows.'

'Aye.' Lennox bobbed his obese head, then said, 'I
know this place. We – er – we use it a lot. Naturally.
There's a refectory. A serve-yourself place, used by the
nurses and such. Tea, coffee, sandwiches . . . that sort o'
thing. It'll be deserted at this hour. Bound to be. I think
we should have a talk, squire. Just you and me. You
deserve to know. And it ain't gonna be easy, old son. It
ain't gonna be at all easy.'

Kim Clarke slept.

Insomnia in this day and age is old-hat. Lullaby cap-
sules have chased insomnia into the medical history books
along with consumption, scurvy and rickets. You want to
sleep? Okay, sleep, by courtesy of Therapharm, Ciba,
Wyeth, Astra and any one of a score of other top-class
drug manufacturers.

Thus, Kim Clarke.

Like her father, she had the full expanse of a double-
bed for her slumber. Like her father, her choice would
have been to have had it otherwise.

For Richard Sullivan the small hours of that morning of
July 30th were a time for mental stock-taking; a time
when sleep was of secondary importance to the business
of gathering together the various strands and figuring
whether the trawl of years had picked up anything of
which he might be justifiably proud.

The rank of deputy chief constable?

Well, they didn't come a-penny-a-box, but on the
other hand he'd known quite a few deputy chief con-

stables. Some good, most of 'em pretty ordinary and a handful he wouldn't have paid in old washers. So which sort was he? That was one hell of a question because from past experience he knew that to a man the lousy ones had all counted themselves as God's gift to the police service. Self-assessment in this field was out. The number of arrests, the scan of the various cases, the umpteen convictions : these were poor guide-lines. Successful coppering demanded luck : the luck to be at the right place at the right time; the luck to hold the rank required to interrogate the villain who was going to crack; the luck to ask the sixty-four-thousand-dollar question to the one person capable of supplying the sixty-four-thousand-dollar answer. Luck all along the line. Application? Certainly, application went without saying, but Sullivan could have named dozens of men, all of whom applied themselves unstintingly to the profession of law-enforcement, but none of whom had yet fingered that all-important touchstone of luck.

Sullivan climbed the stairs to the first floor of Lessford M.P.D. Headquarters.

The Operations-Centre-cum-Recreation-Room was ticking over.

Just that. The room itself seemed to be snoozing, cat-napping while it had the chance and before the urgencies, which were part of a major crime enquiry, jerked it into near-chaotic activity. Before filing, referencing and cross-referencing had men and women jostling each other across its polished floor. Before the trestle-tables threatened to overspill with paper. Before the typewriters clacked and the telephone bells rang and the traffic of the enquiry kept the swing-doors forever opening and closing. Before the two blackboards became a mass of names and instructions, and the notice-board was filled with typed rotas and photostats of blown-up street-maps.

It was all there. The man-hunting machine. Ready for

somebody to press the button and start it humming. Meanwhile it rested, tended by three sleepy-eyed uniformed clerks and an under-employed detective inspector.

As Sullivan entered the D.I. screwed his cigarette into a tin ash-tray and walked across the room to greet the deputy chief constable.

'Dammit, they shoulda let me *know*.'

'Easy, old son.'

Weariness fought heartbreak for possession of Wrie's brain and the agony of the battle dulled his eyes and slurred his speech a little.

'We haven't much brass. Not all *that*. But we've t' house, an' a few quid in t' bank. We'd have . . .'

'It wouldn't have helped,' murmured Lennox.

'Ten thousand bloody quid. My lad's life. My God, where's their priorities? Eh? Tell me that. Where's their *priorities*?'

Lennox hoisted himself from the chair. He waddled across the deserted refectory, busied himself with the tea-and-coffee machine, then returned to the table carrying two carton-cups of steaming sweet tea.

As he sat down, he said, 'This is part of it that *isn't* a "bobby's job".'

'Eh?' Wrie frowned forced concentration across the table.

'Telling people like you,' rumbled Lennox. 'Telling 'em. Not wanting to hurt 'em. But hurting 'em like hell.'

'Oh! . . . Aye.'

Wrie put out a hand, robot-like and apparently without conscious thought. He lifted the carton-cup to his lips, sipped tea, then replaced the cup on the table.

Lennox sipped at the second cup, then said, 'Your missus'll be wanting you, old son.'

'She's at her sister's place.'

'Aye, you said. She'll still be wanting you.'

Wrie hesitated, then muttered, 'Will they . . .?' then stopped.

Lennox waited. He knew what was coming, but he waited.

'Will they . . .?' Wrie swallowed, then said, 'be cutting him up?'

'They won't mark him,' promised Lennox.

'Dammit, they know . . .'

'No.' Lennox shook his head. 'To you. To me. But the law – the coroner – they have to be sure. Very sure.'

Wrie's voice was flat and without a trace of emotion when he said, 'Tha knows what? Cold-blooded bastards. Every last one of you. My lad an' you don't give a damn. Cold-blooded bastards, that's what.'

Lennox might not have heard.

He said, 'Finish your tea, old son. Your missus'll be wanting you. You'll be needing each other for a while.'

They stood on the landing outside the Operations-Centre-cum-Recreation-Room. Sullivan, a deputy chief constable, and Tallboy, a detective inspector, recently promoted from the rank of detective sergeant. The gap in age could have made them father and son. The gap in rank was on a par with that of bishop and curate. Nevertheless these gaps were spanned without conscious effort by either man.

There was a very simple reason. Tallboy's wife was called Susan, Susan Tallboy, and before that Susan Goodright. Goodright, too, had been a detective sergeant, in the old county constabulary, and some years ago (one Christmas, of all times) Susan Goodright had known the pain of becoming a policeman's widow. Goodright had died a particularly painful death in the course of his duty on the snow-covered 'tops' of the wild moorlands. She'd taken it badly, but she might have taken it much worse had it not been for the fact that, in addition to being a

74

copper's wife, she was also a copper's daughter. The daughter of Charles Ripley. The by now legendary Ripley, chief superintendent of the old Beechwood Brook Division of the county area.

Ripley in the county. Sullivan, holding a chief-superintendentship in Lessford City. The two men had worked together too many times for there not to be a bond. They had been, as Mary Sullivan had remarked earlier, remarkably alike : in thought, in methods, in bloody-mindedness. They'd been firm friends and Sullivan knew Susan and counted her almost as his own daughter. He'd known Goodright, and known Goodright to be a good husband. He knew Tallboy and knew that, if anything, Tallboy was an even better husband, and certainly a better copper.

Hence, despite the difference in rank and difference in age, the easy rapport between the two men. Sullivan smoked his pipe, Tallboy smoked a cigarette, and they talked in low voices and the words they spoke had under-the-surface meanings which both understood, but neither mentioned.

'Quiet,' observed Sullivan.

'Yeah. The big push comes tomorrow.'

'With the *Tribune*.'

'Seen a copy?' asked Sullivan.

'Uhuh.' Tallboy nodded. 'That editorial's bad enough. But it's two-edged. It's news, too. They've let the reporter run wild. "John Doe". The lot.'

'Us?'

'No. Kingsley's kept his mouth shut. I think he fancies himself as some sort of martyr.'

'Still . . .' Sullivan moved his shoulders.

'Yeah,' agreed Tallboy. 'They'd be out for blood if they knew.'

'The good old British public.' The observation had a sour sound.

Tallboy drew on the cigarette, then said, 'Sticky, though, if they found out.'

'They'll find out,' growled Sullivan.

'I don't see . . .'

'A thing like that. You can keep it under wraps for only so long, Chris.'

'Yeah.' Tallboy accepted the use of his Christian name without surprise. Off duty they knew each other well enough for first names. On duty it was Sullivan's privilege if he wished to use it. Tallboy said, 'Let's hope he's inside before it leaks.'

'There'll be resignations,' said Sullivan, glumly.

'Oh, I dunno.'

'Somebody, somewhere, will want his pound of flesh. Bet your pension on it.'

'The hell!' Tallboy was suddenly exasperated. 'We work our nuts off. And for a pittance. And what happens? We make a mistake – a wrong reckoning – something anybody could do and some smooth-talking hound uses it as a bandwagon.'

'Every time,' agreed Sullivan.

'Don't *they* ever make mistakes?'

'Sure.'

'Is that justice?'

'We're not talking about justice, Chris. We're talking about bobbying.' Sullivan grinned wryly and added, 'Anyway, this damn force is top-heavy. A few resignations wouldn't come amiss.'

Tallboy said, 'I can't think of anybody.'

'Oh, I can.' Sullivan's smile became even more cynical. 'Shaft-horses, too old to pull their weight.'

'For "age" read "experience",' countered Tallboy. 'That's something beyond price.'

'Today?'

'Especially today.'

'It's all by the book,' muttered Sullivan. 'Get the

chapter and verse right. Nobody complains about whether the villains end up where they belong. Whether they still walk the streets.'

'That's not true.' Tallboy watched the older man's eyes as he spoke. 'Sugden, Lenny, Harris, yourself. Blayde and Sweetapple among the uniformed crowd. Christ, this force wouldn't be the same, without.'

'I'm not suggesting a mass exodus,' said Sullivan, drily.

'Just one,' insisted Tallboy. 'We'd feel the difference.'

They talked. Each knew what the other meant, that the generalities masked specifics and that the abstracts were in fact concretes. The way bobbies talk when they can't bring themselves to voice their true thoughts. The way friends talk.

SATURDAY – JULY 30th

Morning . . .

For a July morning it was a poor thing. A washout. A dawn which gave promise of one more day in a summer which was both wet and disappointing. Overhead the clouds were solid and gunmetal grey, the impression was it would rain forever. And not even *rain*, not even a full-blooded downpour. Instead a haze of moisture which seemed to drift and cling and make the whole world soggy and miserable.

The vans carrying the post-dawn deliveries of *The Lessford and Bordfield Tribune* zig-zagged the near-deserted streets and their tyres made an endless sibilation on the soaked tarmac.

In the Operations-Centre-cum-Recreation-Room Tall-boy organised the emptying of ash-trays, the washing-up of used cups, the sweeping of the floor and the opening of the windows, in order to get the fug and grime of the night dispersed.

Elsewhere in the headquarters building early-shift men stretched and yawned prior to another day, ran battery-operated electric razors over their overnight stubble and cleansed the last of the night from their mouths with the first mug of hot, sweet tea. The cleaners arrived to sweep and polish. The first post was delivered and a duo of cadets sorted out the various envelopes and parcels. Squad-car drivers took delivery of vehicles from their night-shift colleagues, checked petrol and mileage, initial-led service sheets, reported 'on duty' via the cars' radios.

Foot-patrol men glanced through the flimsies covering police activity since last they were on duty, jotted down the numbers of stolen cars in their notebooks, saw without surprise that 'the big 'un', the murder enquiry, had moved no nearer to a solution.

Like a reluctant flexing of muscles by a fighter who has entered the ring scores of times before, law-enforcement prepared itself for one more battle. Another day, one day nearer the pension.

To an untrained observer there might have seemed even a hint of boredom about it all.

8 a.m.

The killer picked up the newspaper from where it had been pushed through the letter-box. As he wandered into the kitchen to await the boiling of the kettle, prior to tea and toast, he unfolded it and read the editorial.

THE APOLOGY WHICH IS TWENTY-FOUR HOURS TOO LATE

It was, he thought, a pity, a criminal waste of human life. The youth, Stephen Wrie, need not have died had somebody, somewhere, had an ounce of humanity. Money, the root of evil, had claimed its usual pride of place. The stuff of which failure and bankruptcy was made had once more worked its own peculiar evil.

And now of course the police would know. They would have the letter. Possibly even the envelope. Clues. No fingerprints, he'd been careful to leave no fingerprints, but, or so he understood, typewriters could be traced via their own 'fingerprints' of typeface.

He read the editorial.

*This then is an unreserved, but we realise quite use-
less, apology. We publish it with the humble assurance,
to all our readers, that we have learned our lesson.*

He smiled to himself. 'To all our readers', but specifically to *one* reader. It was a pity that Stephen Wrie had
had to die. A pity, but necessary. People would now take
things seriously.

The kettle boiled and steam gushed from the spout and
rattled the lid. The killer re-folded the newspaper, placed
it on the seat of a kitchen chair and brewed tea. He
wondered whether tea, or coffee, was the accepted
domestic beverage in Moose Jaw.

Sugden was relieving Lennox as the 'commander in the
field' of the murder hunt. Sugden from Lessford, Lennox
from Bordfield . . . and it was a nice bonus that 'Lenny'
was splitting the twenty-four-hour period with the two
assistant chief constables (crime), rather than Rucker, the
Lessford head of C.I.D. and Lennox's opposite number.
With 'Lenny' you could relax your stays, let your bollocks hang loose and not be forever waiting for the snide
remark. Sugden had all the time in the world for Lennox;
the subtle art of one-up-manship had no part in the
pudgy detective's make-up.

Sugden touched the fresh tobacco in the bowl of his
pipe with a match flame and between puffs said,
'Nothing hectic, I hope. Nothing likely to need the
Brigade of Guards.'

'Old man Wrie's back.' Lennox rubbed the nape of his
neck and stretched some of the tiredness from his fat
frame. 'He's seen the lad. Identified him. We'll need a
statement. Later, I think, when he's got used to the idea.'

'I'll fix it.' Sugden waved out the match.

'Somebody with a bit o' feeling,' warned Lennox. 'At

the moment, he ain't all that keen on coppers.'

Sugden grunted.

Lennox said, 'There's a P.M. at ten. Inquest two-thirty : opened and adjourned, for sure.'

'For sure,' agreed Sugden.

'And,' said Lennox, 'it might not be a bad idea to have somebody on duty at the *Tribune* office. Seen today's issue?'

'He'll come again,' said Sugden. 'That bloody editorial's asking for it.'

'Winnie's idea.'

'It's living dangerously,' complained Sugden.

'What else?' Lennox blew out his cheeks and made them even fatter. 'Some sorta lead from somewhere.'

'Happen,' conceded Sugden, doubtfully.

'And o' course, the barmpots.'

'By the cartload,' sighed Sugden.

'So-o, somebody at the *Tribune*. Eh?'

'Preston,' suggested Sugden.

'Aye.' Lennox nodded.

'It'll get him from under everybody's feet.'

'They'll love him,' chuckled Lennox.

'And Rucker chasing the paper in the Recreation Room.'

Lennox nodded, and said, 'It'll keep 'em apart.'

'Why the hell . . .?' began Sugden, then stopped.

Lennox answered the unasked question. He said, 'The boss. Gilliant. Preston was an obvious choice. So was Newton. And Peirce. All up and coming detective super-intendents. It might have made for bad blood. Do a hop-skip-and-jump. Flip Rucker past all three of 'em. Now, they've stopped hating each other. They're all too busy hating Rucker.'

'And that *doesn't* make for bad blood?'

'Rucker loves it.' The fat detective grinned. 'It's what the old devil lives for.'

The first crank call was logged in, to the minute. It was fed into the M.P.D. headquarters' switchboard, then hurriedly transferred to the Operations-Centre-cum-Recreation-Room. A woman police constable took the call, listened to the first few words, then said, 'If you'll wait a minute, please. I have a Chief Detective Superintendent Rucker, here. I think it's him you want to speak to.'

She handed the receiver to Rucker and held her breath for a few minutes. It was possible, just possible. It might be *him*.

Rucker said, 'Rucker.'

'Who?'

'Rucker. Detective Chief Superintendent Rucker. The policewoman who answered the call put the cart before the horse. Women make a habit of doing that sort of thing.'

The woman police constable stopped holding her breath and glared.

The voice said, 'Are you the big man in this thing?'

'Height, weight or authority?' asked Rucker, softly.

'Eh?'

'The word "big". It means nothing.'

'In charge?'

'I'm as high as you're going to get,' Rucker assured the voice.

'Don't get cocky.'

'Once more, and I hang up,' promised Rucker.

'I'm John Doe.'

Rucker purred, 'I don't give a damn if you're Jack the Ripper. Tell *me* not to get cocky any more, and you'll be talking to a dead mouthpiece.'

'I want ten thousand,' said the voice.

'Don't we all.'

'Otherwise, you've another dead 'un on your hands.'

'We have a very large mortuary.'

'I mean it,' said the voice, harshly.

Rucker said, 'I doubt if you could pull that sort of a shot again.'

'I can handle a gun.'

'You're pretty unique. Not many men can use a .45 revolver with that degree of accuracy.'

'Ask Wrie.'

'It was a lucky shot,' sneered Rucker.

'I did it. Easy. I can handle a forty-five, all right. You'll see.'

'Fine.' Rucker allowed a smile to touch his lips. He drawled, 'As a personal favour. Take the revolver, shove it as far as possible up your anus. Then squeeze the trigger as many times as possible, before the bullets come out of the top of your head.'

He replaced the receiver.

The woman police constable stammered, 'Wasn't it? – I mean . . .'

'Oh, dear me, no.' Rucker cocked a sardonic eyebrow. 'They'll come, like leaves in autumn, miss. Oh, and – er – get it right, next time. *Detective* chief superintendent. The rank of "chief detective" is one used by our American cousins, they don't know any better.'

The woman police constable swallowed, and murmured, 'Yes, sir.'

9.25 a.m.

A man and his daughter; a killer and his only child. The man knelt on a hassock in one of the rear pews of a deserted church and talked to his God. The daughter wheeled a trolley along the aisles of a supermarket and talked with a neighbour.

'Dear God, give me strength of purpose. Let me not weaken in this, my only way back to self-respect.'

'And soap. Have you seen how expensive that is, these days? It's almost doubled in price in the last year.'

'Give me the will. Give me the courage. Be with me, if I weaken.'

'And washing-powder, too.'

'Our Father, which art in heaven.'

'Mind you, I do what my mother used to do.'

'Hallowed be Thy name.'

'She saved pounds, by using old bits of soap.'

'Thy kingdom come.'

'Any odd bit of soap. Toilet soap. Carbolic soap. The odd scraps you usually throw away.'

'Thy will be done.'

'You just flake it, with an old knife. Flake it as thinly as possible.'

'In earth, as it is in Heaven.'

'Into a pail. An old basin. Something like that.'

'Give us this day our daily bread.'

'Then you pour boiling water over it. Not too much. About twice, or three times, as much water as you have soap shavings.'

'Forgive us our trespasses, as we forgive those who trespass against us.'

'Then you leave it to cool and to set.'

'And lead us not into temptation.'

'It comes out a jell. Like blancmange.'

'But deliver us from evil.'

'Then if you take a cupful, not quite a cupful, and put it in the machine with your clothes.'

'For Thine is the kingdom, the power and the glory.'

'It's every bit as good as washing powder, I'm sure.'

'For ever and ever.'

'And it's pure soap. It really *cleans* the clothes.'

'*Amen.*'

'As good as washing-powder. Better, I think. And, of course, it doesn't cost anything.'

The man rose to his feet, dusted the knees of his trousers and walked slowly from the church.

The woman wheeled her trolley to one of the cash-out desks and sorted notes and coins from her purse.

The business of a murder enquiry. Indeed, the business of every major crime. Manpower; its limitations and the best way to use it.

Sugden, being wise in the ways of various law-enforcement techniques, used the manpower available well. Two hundred coppers (thereabouts), and a hunt which had no real spoor. They had a corpse, they had a bullet, they had a letter and they had an envelope. And that's *all* they had.

Start with a proposition. That the envelope and the letter were directly associated with the corpse and the bullet. That the corpse and the bullet were there because the envelope and the letter had been ignored. Ergo, you had a comedian who had in effect come up with a new angle; not 'Your money or your life' but instead, 'Your money or *a* life.' Anybody's life. Man, woman or child. A straight choice . . . loot or a corpse.

But what of the other proposition? The possibility of a coincidence?

That the envelope and the letter were *not* associated with the corpse and the bullet. That some nutter had typed the letter and addressed the envelope, whereas *another* nutter had corpsed young Wrie. In which case you forgot the envelope and the letter, and concentrated all your energies upon the corpse and the bullet.

It was a two-horse race, and Sugden had to back both nags.

Sugden knew his detectives.

He knew that jacks come in three distinct shades. The 'hunch men', the 'lead men' and the 'snout men'. Overlaps occur; 'hunch men' sometimes follow leads and often have snouts; 'lead men' sometimes, but very rarely, have hunches and they too have snouts; 'snout men' enjoy the periodic hunch and have been known to follow leads. But, by and large, the triple route to a successful conviction is, like a three-lane carriageway, marked out by specific guide-lines.

Sugden sent the 'lead men' out, following the second proposition : that the envelope and letter were unrelated to the bullet and the corpse. The 'hunch men' he allowed to follow their noses, on the assumption that the man who had sent the letter had also sent the bullet. The 'snout men' he let run wild; grubbing around the 'grass' of the criminal fraternity, in the hope that somebody, somewhere, would give a firm direction along which the enquiry might be steered.

They worked in pairs; a detective, accompanied by a uniformed man, in plain clothes. The overspill from the uniformed branch he used on the continued house-to-house enquiries; the last hat from which any rabbit might be produced, but something which the rate- and tax-payers expected and, therefore, something which the rate- and tax-payers had to be given.

The business of a murder enquiry.

In its initial stages, organised guesswork.

10.40 a.m.

Richard Wrie said, 'You'll be Muriel, I reckon.'

The girl who had opened the door to his ring nodded.

'I'm Stephen's father.'

'Oh!'

'I'd like to come inside. D'you mind?'

She opened the door a little wider, and stood aside for him to pass in front of her.

It was an odd meeting. Peculiar. Macabre. On the face of it, the only thing they had in common was a recent death : the violent death of his son and her lover. And yet there was an instant homogeneity. There was a shared heartbreak, a shared sense of shock and a shared loss. But there was something else. Something difficult to describe, and yet something very real; something not too far removed from an internal fury, an inner rage against fate itself. Both were pale and carried that crumpled appearance which is a by-product of sleeplessness and emotional stress. The girl's eyes were swollen and red from crying.

The man removed his hat as he entered the tiny flatlet. His gaze took in the pathetic bits and pieces which went to make up this last 'home' of his dead son. A quick frown of near-disapproval flickered across his face as his eyes touched, then left, the divan bed.

He seemed to settle his feet more firmly on one of the mats, before he said, 'You'll have . . .' He cleared his throat, then completed the sentence. 'You'll have heard, I reckon?'

She nodded. Jerkily. Mouth tightly compressed, as if refusing exit to some great scream of pain.

Wrie muttered, 'We're . . . His mother, and me. Especially his mother. This.' He moved the hat in his hand in a tiny circular gesture, which included the flatlet and everything it contained. 'We weren't . . . y'know.'

'We loved each other,' she whispered.

'Aye.' He nodded, miserably.

'Sit down, Mr. Wrie.' Her voice was soft, but harsh. Like a badly-used and over-played gramophone record. 'Please sit down.'

'Aye.'

He moved towards the divan bed, then stopped and seemed to shy away from it. He turned and folded himself on to one of the gaily-painted kitchen chairs.

He said, 'You'll have seen . . . Y'know. This morning's *Tribune.*'

'Why?' she asked and, as she spoke the word, her bottom lips started to tremble. The tears spilled over and ran down her cheeks. 'Why Steve?'

'Nay.' Wrie shook his head in slow bewilderment. His out-of-focus eyes stared at a point on the floor beyond his feet. 'Tha mu'n ask somebody else that, lass. Why *my* lad? I've been asking t' same question. Ever sin' they told us.'

'I'm – I'm sorry,' she murmured, and the tears streamed down her face unheeded.

'Aye. That's what they all say. Sorry. Sympathy. Damn words . . . that's all. Damn *words*!'

'What can I . . .?' She moved her hands, helplessly. 'I *am* sorry, Mr. Wrie. For you, I mean. For Mrs. Wrie. I – *I* loved him, too.'

'Happen.'

'He – he lived here. We were . . . We were . . . *married*. Married, if you like. Husband and wife, if that's how you want to put it. We were . . .'

'Aye.' Wrie raised his head, and looked at her face. 'Married . . . I reckon. Maybe t' certificate doesn't mean all it used to mean. Maybe if t' feeling's there, that's t' main thing. I've known some rare marriages. If that's being "married", happen your way's t' best. I dunno. I know nowt, since they told us. I dunno why I've come. Here. To this place. Happen I just wanted to see. Y'know . . . to *see*. What it was he thowt so much about. This place he called "home". He seemed to treasure it more than his *real* home. Happen that's why. Why I'm here.'

88

'It was his home,' she said, gently. 'It was *our* home.'

'Aye . . . happen. Happen.'

Meanwhile, the gentle people – the pixilated folk – were drawn to police stations, in their bemused cravings for notoriety.

Old Meg, for example.

God knows how old she was: fifty, sixty, even seventy. She looked a hundred and seventy; her face was like a particularly badly treated prune; battered, lined, wrinkled and weather-browned, until the pinched lines of her mouth continued into the lips, and the colouring of lips and face gave no real clue as to where one ended and the other began.

Every copper in Sopworth knew Old Meg. In a back-to-front sort of way she was a mascot. In one respect she represented something they would never have. Complete freedom. The great and munificent welfare state wanted no part of Old Meg; nor, come to that, did Old Meg give a fig for the welfare state. It was her life and she lived it her way.

A couple of centuries previously she'd have been burned at the stake as a witch, and some of the more susceptible coppers of Sopworth still weren't too damn sure!

In winter she slept her nights away huddled in the warmth of the cooling kilns of the brickworks which flanked Sopworth. In summer it was Dutch barns or cattle-byres. She stole food from the market, milk from the doorsteps and, it was rumoured, clothes from the scarecrows. In this she was a thief, but she was tolerated as a harmless thief; she never stole money or valuables because she had no use for money or valuables. The farmers and brickworks labourers fed her a little. The do-gooders of the parish hounded her, whenever they lacked some other worthy target for their imposed philanthropy,

and were cursed to the high heavens for their inter-
ference.

She was Old Meg. One day she'd die, she'd be found
dead, in a barn or a kiln, and Sopworth would be that
much less colourful. Meanwhile she shuffled through life.
Independent and monumentally filthy. Bent and racked
with aches and pains which would have stretched lesser
women on a hospital bed. Cunning and full of guile and,
in some strange way, 'knowledgeable'. Nobody had
ever seen her read a book or a newspaper. Nobody
had ever seen her read, period. Certainly she never listened to a radio or watched a television set. And yet, she
knew. Everything that happened in and around Sopworth
was Old Meg's personal concern. And, if possible it
demanded a trudge to the police station, followed by a
solemn-faced 'confession'.

She walked crab-like to the public counter, and the
middle-aged constable on station duty heaved a sigh of
resignation.

'I did it,' she crooned.

'Aye. I don't doubt it, Meg.'

'It were needed, weren't it?' She hawked phlegm from
the back of her throat, and the constable winced as a
blast of bad breath hit him straight in the face. She
amplified, 'I mean, 'im being what 'e was. It were
needed.'

'If you say so.'

'Rotten boogers like 'im . . . eh?'

'Off you go, Meg.' The constable fished a 10p piece
from his pocket, and placed it on the counter top. He
said, 'Away, and buy yourself a cuppa tea.'

She was suddenly very angry. She spat at the coin,
and a spray of spittle bespattered the polished surface.

She almost screamed, 'I di'n do it for reward. I di'n
do it for money.'

'All right, Meg. Cool off.'

'I di'n do it for *that*.'

'No. Of course you didn't.'

'I did it 'cos 'e were a rotten booger.'

'Aye. There's a lot of 'em about,' said the constable, sadly.

'I'll get 'em, though . . . eh?' The anger left her, and she grinned black and broken teeth. 'I'll get 'em all . . . eh?'

'In time,' agreed the constable.

'D'you know 'ow?' She cocked a head, sparrow-fashion. 'Eh? D'you know 'ow?'

'Meg . . . "' began the constable, wearily.

'I just thowt it. Y'know, just thowt it. An' that's all. That's 'ow it were done. I thowt, 'e's a rotten booger. Better wi'out. An' that's all. That's 'ow it were done.'

'You're a clever lass, Meg,' soothed the constable. 'Now . . .'

'An' you're another.' She glared up at him.

'Eh?'

'A rotten booger.' She spat at the coin again. 'Givin' me *that*. I di'n do it for that.'

'No. All right. Just . . .'

'Best be careful, eh? Best look out. You're another. A rotten booger. Best look out, just in case.'

She turned and shuffled her way out of the police station.

The constable watched her, eyed the moistened 10p piece, then shook his head in mild disgust.

He murmured, 'God Almighty! People wouldn't believe.'

And yet some they did believe. At least for a time.

One of them walked through the revolving doors of *The Lessford and Bordfield Tribune* offices, approached

91

the counter signed 'Enquiries' and patiently waited until the lady clerk had ended her telephone conversation with some unseen colleague.

The clerk looked up and saw an elderly man, well dressed in brown tweed and wearing a matching tweed cap. The face was full and slightly florid and the white, carefully trimmed moustache went with the bearing to give an immediate impression of retired militarism. The man had a golf-bag slung over his right shoulder.

The clerk smiled, and said, 'Yes, sir?'

'The editor, please.'

Again, the polite authority gave more than a hint of the Parade Ground and the Orderly Room.

'Have you an appointment?' asked the clerk.

'No.'

'In that case, I'm sorry. I'm afraid . . .'

'Tell him, John Doe.'

'John . . .' The clerk stared, open-mouthed and wide-eyed.

'John Doe.' The man smiled what can only be described as a crusty smile, and added, 'Don't worry, m'dear. It's all over now.'

'Y-yes, sir.' The clerk felt for the receiver, without taking her eyes from the man's face. She spoke to the switchboard. 'The – the editor's office. As quickly as you can, please.' She waited, still watching the man's face, then said, 'Mr. – Mr. Kingsley. It's the Enquiry Desk here. There's a – there's a man. John Doe. He says he's John Doe. He – he wants to see you, Mr. Kingsley.' She replaced the receiver, and stammered, 'He'll be down, Mr. Doe. He'll – he'll be down, immediately.'

'Thank you.' The man nodded stiff gratitude, hitched the golf-bag more firmly on to his shoulder and waited.

Kingsley and Preston arrived at the front office a little breathless, having raced down the three flights of stairs.

Kingsley arrived at the Enquiry Desk fractionally ahead of Preston.

The man turned, and said, 'Ah. Are you . . . ?'

'Preston.' Preston beat Kingsley to the punch. 'Police. Detective superintendent.'

'Good.' The man moved his head in slow satisfaction. 'In that case . . .'

'John Doe? That who you claim to be?'

'A pseudonym, of course.'

'But that's who you claim to be?' insisted Preston.

'That's who I *am*, superintendent.'

'Good.' Preston took a deep breath, then exhaled it in a long sigh. '*Bloody* good. You – er – you did the right thing.'

'Of course.' The man unslung the golf-bag from his shoulder, and said, 'You'll be needing this.'

'Why? What the hell do I want with a set of . . .'

'The gun.'

'Oh!'

'I couldn't very well carry it through the streets openly.'

Preston almost snatched the bag from the man's grasp. He unzipped the top and there, along with five assorted golf irons, was a rifle.

A group of half-a-dozen front-desk employees had gathered around the trio and more were glancing, with open curiosity, in their direction. There would soon be a small crowd then perhaps passing pedestrians from the street. Kingsley saw the possible danger first.

He said, 'There's a small room . . .'

'Eh?' Preston looked up, from where he was peering into the golf-bag.

'It's over there.' Kingsley nodded toward a door leading from the larger public hall. 'We keep it for anybody who wants to check on past editions. I think we'd be better . . .'

93

'Aye. A lot better.' Preston turned to the elderly man and said, 'Right, Sunny Jim. Let's have you in there. There's some questions need asking.'

10.45 a.m.

The killer locked the doors of his car and fed a 10p piece into the parking meter. He was a Lessford man; he knew Bordfield, as most inhabitants of the two cities knew both places, but like most other citizens of the area, he had an affinity with one and counted the other city as being, in some strange way, inferior.

The six months or so since he'd last been there had seen some changes. The shopping precinct, for example. What had once been a sea of churned earth sprouting scaffolding, cranes, civil-engineering equipment and hap-hazardly-positioned concrete blocks was now a miniature 'Bull Ring'; a deliberately contrived take-off of Birmingham's bull's-eye centre-piece. But wrong and stupid-looking, because it was so Lilliputian; the proportions had a strange effect upon the shoppers; they gave the impression of a world in which giants strolled along paved and silent walkways.

The killer felt hemmed-in. Trapped in some miniaturised, soft-footed Bedlam. The Saturday shoppers, but without the Saturday traffic. It was wrong. Unnatural. Frightening. An echoing jungle transplanted into the very heart of a busy city. And the effect was heightened by the massive, concrete bowls in which the parks department had planted an array of growing flowers and shrubs.

The killer sought the reassurance of traffic noise then, his hint of panic gone, he entered a telephone kiosk.

Again the call went through the switchboard to the Operations-Centre-cum-Recreation-Room. Again the woman police constable took the call and handed it on to Rucker.

Rucker spoke into the mouthpiece and said, 'Are you another one?'

'Another what?'

'Relieve yourself, little man,' sneered Rucker. 'Get it all out of your system, then go back to your padded cell.'

'Who *is* that?' demanded the killer.

'Rucker. Detective chief superintendent. And as far as you're going to get with your fairy tales.'

'Fairy tales?'

'I'm a busy man. Not a patient man, but a busy man. I'm expected to listen to fools like you. But only for so long.'

'This is John Doe,' said the killer.

'Of course you are. Isn't everybody this morning?'

'I mean it.'

'Everybody means it.'

'I shot Wrie, yesterday.'

'Everybody shot Wrie, yesterday.'

'I shot him from the Odeon cinema.'

'Of course. From the projection room? Or from the stage?'

'From the toilet window.'

'Good.' Rucker's lips moved into a contemptuous smile.

'I used a .303 rifle.'

'Clev-ver,' mocked Rucker. 'Where do you carry it? In your breast pocket?'

The killer worked hard to make himself be believed. He said, 'Look – whoever you are . . .'

'Rucker. Remember?'

'. . . it takes to pieces.'

'Does it?' Some of the contempt left Rucker's voice. He began to believe.

The killer said, 'Ten pieces. Including the sight and sight-mount.'

'Go on,' said Rucker, carefully.

'That's all.'

'Assuming I believe you,' said Rucker.

'You'd be wise.'

'Why here? Why not the newspaper?'

'It's progressed. Past the newspaper. It belongs to the police now.'

'Indeed.' Rucker clapped a hand over the mouthpiece, glanced at the policewoman and snapped, 'Get this call traced. Fast!' The policewoman hurried toward a second telephone and Rucker continued his conversation with the killer. He murmured, 'Have you run out of postage stamps then?'

'What?'

'The telephone call, you idiot.'

'I need to talk to you.'

'Urgently?' mocked Rucker. He watched the woman police constable talking into the mouthpiece of the second telephone. He said, 'Why not write? We'd love a letter from you. We might even frame it.'

In an angry voice, the killer said, 'You still don't believe me.'

'You're about the tenth,' lied Rucker, smoothly.

'The tenth what?'

'The tenth John Doe.'

'Look . . . I *am* John Doe.'

'And the tenth to say that. It gets monotonous.'

'The price is higher,' said the killer, coldly.

'Bravo.'

'Much higher.'

'How would you like it delivered? Choc-bars? Or Smarties?'

96

'Fifty thousand pounds. You'd better believe that, whoever you are.'

'Rucker. Detective chief superintendent. Make a note of it. Then, you won't have to keep asking.' Rucker covered the mouthpiece and snapped, 'For Christ's sake get this call traced. I can't keep him talking forever.'

The woman police constable gasped, 'Yes, sir. I'm doing my best.'

'Fifty thousand pounds. Used notes. And have them ready by noon tomorrow.'

'Tomorrow is Sunday,' purred Rucker. 'Or have you misplaced your diary?'

'By God! You *still* don't believe me.' The anger of the killer made his voice tremble slightly.

Rucker murmured, 'Right in one, little man. I still don't believe you.'

'Somebody else gets killed,' warned the killer.

'It happens all the time. That, too, gets monotonous.'

'Damn you. *I am John Doe.*'

'John Doe writes letters,' said Rucker.

'And policemen can trace typewriters.'

'Typed . . . of course. You can even read newspapers. You surprise me.'

'All right!' exploded the killer. 'Typed. The address, too, and that wasn't reproduced in this morning's *Tribune.*'

'Clever.'

'Posted at Lessford Central, at half-past one, on Wednesday.'

'No-o,' agreed Rucker, thoughtfully. 'Those bits and pieces weren't reproduced in the *Tribune.*'

'Therefore . . .'

'Therefore you might be.'

'*Might* be?'

'Or a good guesser.'

'Are you mad?' rasped the killer.

'I don't think so. On the other hand, I don't have certification to prove that I'm sane. What about you?'

There was a pause, then the killer said, 'Have the money ready, Rucker . . .'

'You've got it right, this time.'

'. . . Fifty thousand. Used notes. And be at that number, at noon, tomorrow.'

'Little man, I am not used to . . .'

'. . . otherwise there's another corpse, before nightfall.'

The line went dead.

Rucker dropped the receiver on to its rest. In three strides, he was across the room. He snatched the second receiver from the hand of the woman police constable.

'Who the hell am I talking to?' he rasped.

A voice said, 'This is the Telephone Area Office. I don't know what . . .'

'I will tell you "what", little man.' Rucker's voice was back to little more than a whisper and spilling with ominous contempt. He purred, 'I will tell you exactly "what". You were asked to trace a call, being made to another telephone at this office . . .'

'I can't do that without . . .'

'. . . Thanks to your bureaucratic twittering. Thanks to the snail's pace at which you seem to make a very obvious decision. Thanks to the fact that you're a flaming idiot . . .'

'Look. You can't . . .'

'. . . Thanks to *you*, a murderer has just replaced a receiver. We don't know who he is. We don't know where he is. We had him, but you let him go, little man. If it is possible – if it is humanly possible – I shall have the pleasure of slapping a charge around your neck. Obstruction of Police. It may stick. It may not stick. But, by Christ, I'm going to try.'

98

Rucker took a deep breath, then lowered the telephone receiver on to its rest, slowly, gently. As if it might break in his hand.

11 a.m.

Wrie sipped at his beaker of coffee and tried hard to hide his distaste. Wrie did not like coffee; tea was his drink – hot, strong, sweet 'sergeant major's' best – and this mildly bitter beverage had an alien effect upon his tongue he could never get used to. It was, he supposed, the 'right' drink. The 'correct' drink. In the posh restaurants it was always coffee. Never tea. 'Coffee, sir. Black or white?' Aye – well – he'd learned to say 'White'. Not like the first time. 'Black with plenty o' milk.' How the hell was *he* to know? A different language. A different way of life. A different culture.

That's what Steve would have said. 'A different culture, Dad. Not better. Not worse. But different.'

Maybe, maybe not. But some things were the same.

Heartbreak, for example. This lass; he'd been 'her' Steve, just as he'd been 'his' Steve. Different relationships, but relationships that touched once you got down under the surface. Steve. The rest didn't matter. Morality, immorality; youth and age; his generation and their generation. What the hell did all that crap matter now?

He muttered, 'I'm – y'know . . . sorry we didn't get to know each other better, when . . .' He choked, then whispered, 'Y'know.'

She nodded and the tears threatened to spill down her cheeks again.

'It's allus too damn late.' His voice was harsh and savage. Low, but weighed with helpless fury. 'Our Steve . . . God, he wanted us to be friends. You an' his mother.

99

An' me. He damn near went on his knees for it. More than once.' He looked at her, shook his head slowly and, in a tone which threatened never to allow him rest, he muttered, 'I'm sorry, lass. It's too late, but I'm sorry.'

The man whose name was Major Chartwell (Retired) said, 'It's all modern youth deserves.'

'For Christ's sake!' snarled Preston. 'Are you round the twist?'

'That's the reason,' said Chartwell. 'Take it or leave it.'

The room was all wrong for this sort of interview. It was pokey, dark and had a faint smell of dust and old newsprint. There was a sloping bench of polished oak against one wall, a sort of stand-up desk on which the bound editions of *The Lessford and Bordfield Tribune* could be rested while their contents were scrutinised. There was a small-paned, dull-glassed window above the desk. The other three walls were fitted with deep shelves on which were stored each year's bound volume of local news and current affairs. Something from Dickens; Scrooge's parlour, for example. Or, if not that, a room in the chambers of some old-fashioned solicitor's office, a place of legal dust and forensic nit-picking.

A most unsuitable place for this trio; this bad-tempered detective superintendent, this wretched-looking editor of a provincial newspaper and this ex-military man, who so wanted to be believed.

There was a tall, leather-padded stool which Preston had dragged from its place under the slope of the shelf-desk. Preston was squatted on this stool. The other two men stood, awkwardly and (or so it seemed) embarrassingly close to each other in the confines of the tiny room.

'Major,' said Kingsley, joylessly, 'that's no reason for

killing a stranger. That you're out of step with modern youth.'

'They're louts.'

'Not all.'

'You people – you press people – you report their vandalisms. Their behaviour at football matches. The way they behave towards decent members of the public. You, of all people . . .'

'And the Proms?' suggested Kingsley, with a sigh. 'And all the voluntary welfare work they do? For pensioners? For the disabled? For . . .'

'Cut the Hearts and Flowers,' interrupted Preston, harshly. 'The old fool didn't shoot Wrie because he hates teenagers. He didn't shoot Wrie, period.'

'You have the gun, superintendent,' said Chartwell.

'No. We have *a* gun. We also have a doddering old clown, who should have more sense.'

'Superintendent . . .” began Kingsley.

'A Winchester,' insisted Preston.

Chartwell said, 'Specifically, superintendent, a Winchester, Model 95, lever action carbine.'

'Which did not fire the bullet which killed Wrie.'

'I say it did.'

'But I'm right,' growled Preston. 'Our ballistics boys don't make mistakes.'

FLATHEAD COUNTY LIBRARY
KALISPELL, MONTANA

'If they can tell . . .'

'They can tell,' chipped in Preston. 'They can prove you're a liar, faster than you can pull that bloody trigger, man. Now, let's stop arsing around and tell some truth for a change. First question . . . who owns the damn gun.'

'I own it,' said Chartwell, wearily. 'Quite legally. I have a certificate from your own chief constable. And a licence.'

Chartwell stopped the charade as quietly, as completely, as any man with intelligence might have done.

He'd played his hand, to the best of his ability, but he'd lost. There was no bluff. No bluster. Just an acceptance of fate, which brought a look of self-disgust to his face, but only for a moment.

Preston glared a little, and said, 'You've wasted police time, Chartwell. I have a report to make. They'll ask why, I'd like to be able to tell 'em why.'

Chartwell moved his shoulders resignedly.

'I, too, major,' said Kingsley, in a gentler tone. 'Curiosity, if you like. But why?'

Chartwell hesitated, then gave the ghost of a smile, and spoke to Kingsley.

He said, 'A simple answer, sir. There's nowhere else left to hide. Prison, perhaps. Few other places . . . none that I can think of.'

'Should you hide?'

'I have a son . . .' Again Chartwell hesitated, then he seemed to make a decision, stared at the brown lino on the floor and continued as if reciting well-remembered facts to himself. 'I'm a soldier. All my life. Since before World War Two. Discipline, manliness, decency. The older ideals which, today, seem to count for so little. I can't change. I don't think I'd want to, even if I could. I've had a good life, an interesting life, and, until seven years ago, I shared that life with a good woman. She's dead and for that I'm grateful. She didn't live to see our son suffering – what's the expression? – "cold turkey". A ludicrous expression, sir, for what it means. An utterly inapt expression for a form of self-conflict capable of bettering all but the exceptionally strong-willed. My son, sir, is not strong-willed. Had he been so, he would not now be a dope addict. A so-called "junkie". A so-called "main-liner".

'This . . .' Chartwell moistened his lips. 'This ridiculous make-believe on my part. My apologies, gentlemen. My sincere apologies, for wasting your time with such an outrageous pantomime. I thought I could bring it off. I truly thought so. An officer – a police officer whose name I refuse to divulge – mentioned that Wrie was shot with a .303. That put the idea into my head. An impossible idea. Indeed, a cowardly idea. A .303 – forgive me, superintendent – a .303, at any reasonable, street-fighting range, would pass through the body of the victim. Almost certainly. That was my assumption. I also assumed that the round would flatten itself against brickwork, stonework, something like that.

'It seemed to me . . .' Chartwell sighed, heavily. 'It seemed to me that, such being the case, no ballistic expert could possibly prove that my carbine was *not* the murder weapon.'

'But why?' insisted Kingsley. 'In God's name, *why*?'

'A gesture, sir. Little more than that. A gesture which might – which just *might* – bring about certain desired effects. To be isolated from the rest of the world. That would have been rather nice. To give my son an excuse, of a sort. The son of a convicted murderer . . . who can blame such a son, if he turns to drugs as a form of escape? Stupid? When he's already an addict? Perhaps. But people have short memories, sir. They make ready excuses for weaknesses. Probably because they're weak themselves. It might have worked. I like to think it might have worked. That this ridiculous gesture might have saved my son some slight embarrassment.

'And the last reason? Not a real reason. More of a hope than a reason. His father, a convicted murderer. It might have shocked him into some sort of strength. Some sort of will-power. Enough, perhaps.'

'I have,' growled Preston, 'heard of some damn silly reasons . . .'

'I know, superintendent. I know.' Once more the crooked smile touched Chartwell's lips. 'Y'see, my life –

all my life – it doesn't prepare you for the intricacies of – of . . .'

He was without the required words and he shook his head in defeat.

'The modern world's pro-permissive arguments?' suggested Kingsley.

'That,' agreed Chartwell. 'That's about as near as it can be put.'

Preston's expression showed strange and, for him, unusual indecision. He wiped his lips with the fingers of one hand, and muttered, 'Aye. You, me both.'

'Superintendent?'

Kingsley raised his eyebrows fractionally as he asked the question. A very loaded question; a question whose one word carried a great weight of implied suggestion.

'I dunno.'

Thoughts flickered through Preston's mind. Like the riffled pages of a book, mental pictures came and went at dizzying speed. The countless humiliations engineered by Rucker. The wife who was no wife, but instead a teasing, maddening and forever dissatisfied woman; a woman whom he still loved, but who was incapable of returning that love. The shouting, the swearing which, in the final analysis, was a huge cover-up job, behind which he hid his own bitterness. Preston, the loud-mouthed fool, who was no fool. The lout, who was no lout. The man, trapped and lost, in his own inadequacies.

In a low voice, he repeated, 'I dunno.'

Chartwell said, 'You have a duty, superintendent.'

'A duty,' agreed Kingsley. 'The duty to find a murderer.'

'Aye.' Preston's shoulders sagged. The sigh seemed to shake his whole frame. He pushed himself from the stool and, as he opened the door, he growled, 'I don't have kids, major. If I had – if one of 'em treated me like yours has treated you – I'd boot his arse all the way

through the top of his stupid skull. That's what *I'd* do
. . . but it wouldn't do any good, would it?'

He left the tiny room, walked across to the stairs and
started to climb his way back to Kingsley's office.

And at Upper Drayson, in a very posh house, a man
called Sullivan (who held a very posh rank, in this new
and very posh Metropolitan Police District) was also
finding some very unexpected wasps in his marmalade
pot.

Sullivan had been up all night. Working? We-ell, he
wouldn't exactly call it working. Not *working*. Tooling
around, thinking miserable thoughts. Feeling his age,
maybe. Buggering about, as out of place as an old maid
at a tart's wedding, but that wasn't *working*.

Or was it?

Deputy chief constable. Oh, very highfalutin'. Very
cut-glass and twenty-Players, but what the steaming hell
did it boil down to? Not bobbying. Whatever else, not
bobbying. Bobbying was . . .

Bobbying was something you felt. A gut reaction.
Being one step ahead of the germs; waiting there, with a
big fat grin on your face, when they tripped up over
their own brains. A satisfaction. A nice, warm feeling
which compensated for all the slogging and missed meals
and missed sleep. Waging a war . . . all right, meeting
violence with counter-violence. What the bloody hell
else? The tearaways, the hooligans . . . what the bloody
hell else? Organise a Bible class, maybe? Those bastards
– the hard core of bad bastards – only understood one
thing. Pain. Terror. The punch-up. And that, too, was
bobbying. Getting your head down and going in swing-
ing, and if that's the only argument they understand,
using that argument. And the hell with riot-shields or
shin-pads or boxes over your balls. In there with less men

and less weaponry than they had and *still* knocking ten shades of shit out of 'em!

North End. Oh, my Christ, yes, North End. Those glorious, blood-red days and nights of North End. The division which was, in effect, the force within a force. Before Gilliant. Before the amalgamation. When Lessford had been a city force and North End had been the very arse-hole of that force and he, Sullivan, had been king-pin, with nobody – nobody! – telling him what to do or how to do it.

And the cherry? The prize for all that never-ending fight to keep the lid on?

A deputy-chief-constableship. What else?

'Do you want anything to eat?'

'Eh?' Sullivan dragged his mind from the morass of memories.

'To eat?' Mary Sullivan's tone was very level. Very non-committal. She said, 'You'll be going back, I suppose. On duty.'

'Oh – er . . . yes.'

'Unless you've had breakfast at the canteen. Something during the night?'

'No.'

'In that case . . .'

'Just this beaker of tea. That's all.' Sullivan's tone matched that of his wife's. Completely neutral; neither friendly nor unfriendly. 'I nipped home for a shave and a shower. I'm not hungry. If I get hungry I'll snatch a bite somewhere.'

Mary Sullivan made as if to say something, then changed her mind.

The killer knew he'd made a mistake. Not a big mistake, nothing fatal, nothing from which the police might trace him. But a mistake nevertheless.

He'd stayed at the telephone too long. He'd been

conned by this Rucker character, conned into a prolonged conversation during which time, and no doubt at
all about this, somebody was trying to link two ends of a
telephone wire. Maybe that was why he'd asked for
fifty thousand and not stuck to the original ten. A spon-
taneous demand. He'd certainly never considered increas-
ing the price. Not even as he'd dialled the number. But
something, some animal instinct of self-preservation perhaps, had made him say 'fifty thousand'. Because this
was a pitcher that could be taken to the well just the
once. Thereafter it would be shattered. So fill it to the
brim. Why stick at ten, when it was just as easy to take
fifty?

Nevertheless there'd been the mistake.

Tomorrow he must be more careful. Much more careful. Because tomorrow they'd be ready. Waiting. Everything organised for the big pounce.

Tomorrow he'd have to be *very* careful.

The realisation of how close he'd been, how close he
might have been, to capture brought on the shakes. Not
a lot, but enough to make him pause, light a cigarette,
then let the smoke seep deep into his lungs and soothe
his nerves a little. It made him by-pass the shopping
precinct, keep to the busy streets and shoulder a way
through the Saturday pedestrians. It was safer that way.
To be lost in a crowd. To be one grain of sand on a
whole beach. It was safer that way, much safer.

He reached his car, climbed in and threaded a way
into the steady stream of traffic.

Noon – 6 p.m.

No more than two dozen men knew. Bear wanted it that
way and Gilliant agreed. It was the gently-gently ap-
proach; the eggshell method.

Bear said, 'Keep the pressure up. House-to-house. Leaning on the informants. Bags of action . . . see? The Sunday newspaper lads are getting under our feet. Give 'em feet to get under. The wrong feet. We can do the other thing – the real thing – quietly and with minimal risk of some clown screwing things up.'

And Gilliant agreed.

Gilliant fixed the fifty thousand.

It wasn't difficult. Gilliant and the manager of the Lessford branch of the National Westminster were golfing buddies. They were also fellow-members of the local Round Table. Those two facts made it not merely possible, but ridiculously easy.

A telephone conversation to the bank manager's boss, and the trick was as good as pulled.

The manager, the chief clerk and Gilliant counted the cabbage in the basement of the deserted bank. Alongside the vault door from which the money had been taken.

'It's bulky,' warned the bank manager.

Gilliant crammed money into the zip-topped holdall and said, 'It'll all go in.' He added, 'Unmarked singles and fives. Right?'

'Unmarked notes,' agreed the manager.

The chief clerk said, 'But not the paper bands, holding the hundreds and five-hundreds, they're initialled by the teller who counted them.'

Gilliant nodded.

'That all right?'

'He can't have everything,' said Gilliant, grimly.

Saturday afternoon. Exercise period within the walls of H.M. Prison, Leeds. And the man Clarke, Samuel Clarke, the killer's son-in-law, trudged from nowhere to nowhere and remembered other Saturday afternoons.

Football. The crowds. The strikers and the sweepers,

and the roar which was almost a physical thing, when the ball smashed into the net. He'd be out, soon. Then, maybe a fortune. *Somebody* won the damn fortunes. Somebody. Every week. Littlewoods, Vernons, Copes . . . they all dished out the big cheques, every week. Why not Samuel Clarke?

By God, if only . . .

He'd give the old man a treat. Start from scratch and build up a new firm. Small, but good. More than good, the best. A partnership, this time. Father and son-in-law. Kim would like that. A new start, a new firm . . . and, by Christ, this time all non-union employees. Good men. Craftsmen. Men whose hands were argument enough for a good wage and good working conditions.

One of the screws called, 'Keep moving, Clarke.'

Judas Christ, if only . . .

The inquest lasted less than ten minutes.

The pathologist took the oath, then spouted medical terms of art which only he and the coroner understood. Stephen Wrie was dead. He'd been shot. That's what it boiled down to. That's what the pathologist said, but his training was such that he had to say it in the non-language of his profession. But that's what it meant, and all the long words in the world couldn't blunt the cutting edge of the simple truth.

Richard Wrie gave evidence of identification. He put a name to a corpse. The law demanded it; the law demanded that, even in death, a man must have an identity.

Wrie gave his evidence softly. Aggressively. As if the coroner and his assistant and all the policemen and pressmen present were his sworn enemies.

The coroner, as coroners will, accepted Wrie's attitude with complete equanimity. He was performing the duty of his office; neither condemning nor commiserating.

He listened, stone-faced, asked few questions and made no comments.

He closed the proceedings in a toneless, sing-song voice.

'. . . a verdict of murder by person or persons unknown. If the next-of-kin will please collect the necessary documents from my clerk. Thank you, ladies and gentlemen. This inquest is now closed.'

Lennox moved alongside Wrie.

As the occupants of the tiny court shuffled to their feet and made towards the door, Lennox said, 'The coroner's assistant, old son. That's him, filling out the forms. He'll give you the paperwork. Take it to whoever's dealing with the funeral arrangements. They'll do the rest.'

'Bring him back, happen?' said Wrie, bitterly.

'If we can do anything . . .'

'Aye.' Wrie's eyes took on life. 'Find him. That's all. Find him. Then leave him wi' me for five minutes.'

And of course the 'snout men' continued to make life that little less comfortable for known police informants.

'John Doe.'

'Sorry, sir. It doesn't ring bells.'

'That's not his real name.'

'In that case . . .'

'A legal term.'

'I'm sorry. I don't . . .'

'You get lawyers in here.'

'Sometimes.'

'Often.'

'We-ell, yes. *Fairly* often.'

'Those ears of yours flap a lot.'

'I – er – I hear things.'

'The expression "John Doe", for example.'

'Sir, I don't know anybody called . . .'

'Lawyers use it.'

'Oh!'

'It's their way of saying "the man in the street".'
'I – er – I didn't know that.'
'You listen to the shysters who use this bar.'
'I hear things, sir.'
'Hear things?'
'Yes, sir.'
'But not John Doe?'
'It's a name I haven't heard, sir. An expression I
haven't heard used.'
'No?'
'No, sir.'
'Don't you read newspapers?'
'*The Times*, sir.'
'*The Tribune*?'
'No, sir. Only *The Times*.'
'Get hold of a copy of *The Tribune*. Today's edition.'
'Might I ask why?'
'John Doe. He's in there, with murder attached.'
'Oh!'
'That's how important.'
'I – er – I see.'
'So, don't cop out, okay?'
'I – I like to help in any way poss . . .'
'But no John Doe?'
'No, sir. I give you my assurance.'
'You know which figures to dial, to reach me?'
'Certainly, sir.'
'Ask around. Keep tuned in, okay?'
'As you say, sir.'
'And don't go coy on me. Not on this one.'
'Have I ever let you down, sir? Have I ever not . . .?'
'It has been known.'
'Sir, I assure you, I've always . . .'
'Just listen, then tell. That way we stay friends. Okay?'
'Yes, sir. I'll do my best, sir.'
Police informants. They come in all shades, all sizes

and wearing a multitude of guises. They are not all dirty-raincoated, snivelling little manikins who creep around and talk out of the side of their mouths. Some of them figure it as a civic duty. The 'snout man' doesn't mind. Call it what the hell you like, to him it's still snitching. To him, it ices the cake.

'I take the money,' insisted Rucker, quietly.

Gilliant looked uncertain. Sullivan, Bear, Sugden and Lennox looked distinctly worried. Other men would know before the deadline. Other men would have to know, if the net was to be close-meshed enough to catch the required fish. But, at the moment, the knowledge that John Doe might soon be get-at-able was limited to the six men gathered in Gilliant's office and, the truth was, it was six, rather than five, because Lennox had meandered back to the M.P.D. headquarters from the inquest, had stayed there to chinwag with Sugden and had been present when Gilliant had gathered as many senior officers as possible, in order to up-date them on the latest development.

'Nobody's suggesting you must,' said Gilliant. 'The job has certain, very obvious, built-in dangers. It has to be a purely voluntary thing.'

'Is anybody suggesting I *shouldn't*?' countered Rucker.

'I am,' said Sullivan, bluntly.

The situation bordered upon the ridiculous. The man they were all after – the killer, John Doe – was moving to within grabbing distance. The holdall was there, alongside Gilliant's desk, and, at some time in the very near future, John Doe had, of necessity, to put out a hand and touch. He had to be *that* close. Which, in turn, meant that somebody, some police officer, could be manoeuvred into a position to bring about an arrest.

The glory, by all the rules of the game, belonged to Rucker. And yet Rucker was the wrong man, and

– Rucker excepted – every man in that office knew this.

'You're the wrong man,' growled Sullivan.

'I take that badly, Mr. Sullivan . . . *sir*.'

Rucker put all the contempt, all the insolence, he could muster into the remark. And, with the words went the expression; an expression reserved for horrible things, usually found under upturned stones.

Sullivan's face remained deadpan, as he said, 'You asked a question. I've given you an answer.'

'That *I* shouldn't be the one to make the arrest?'

'I'm not talking about the arrest.'

'I am. With respect, Mr. Sullivan . . . *sir*.'

Sugden said, 'We need somebody with patience, Rucker. That's not your long suit.'

'Patience?' Rucker raised sardonic eyebrows.

Sugden said, 'Don't come the old madam with *me*, superintendent . . .'

'*Chief* superintendent.'

'. . . otherwise, it won't be an explanation, it'll be an order.'

'Chief constable?'

Again, it was a studied insult. A deliberate, and contemptuous dismissal of Sugden's warning. A soft and offensive ignoring of Sugden's rank and position in the force.

Rucker waited, a slow, sarcastic smile playing catch-me-if-you-can at the corners of his mouth.

Gilliant said, 'Mr. Lennox. Your opinion, if you please.'

'We-ell, now.' Lennox rubbed the layers of fat around his jowl, thoughtfully. 'It's old Rucker's prerogative. He baited the trap.'

'The hell he baited the trap,' snapped Sugden. 'He answered a telephone call. Any one of us, any grass-green recruit in the whole force, could have . . .'

'Mr. Sugden. Please.' Gilliant returned his attention to Lennox and said, 'Go on. We're listening.'

'*If* a trap was baited, Rucker baited it,' rumbled the fat detective. 'He was at the right spot, at the right time. That at least. If he's lucky in one thing, he could be lucky in another. But . . .' Lennox grinned. 'Y'see, he *looks* like a copper, don't he? A bit skinny, maybe. But a copper, nothing surer. Now, if His Nibs ain't averse to a copper doing the delivery, why not Rucker? But if he *is*, if he wants some civilian to hoik the loot along, I'd say *not* old Rucker. In that case, I'd say somebody who looks a lot less like a copper. I think we should take it, as it comes. A couple o' bag-carriers at the ready. Rucker. And somebody who just don't look like a flatfoot.'

'You, for instance,' smiled Bear.

'I'd be willing,' said Lennox.

'And, your opinion, Mr. Bear?' asked Gilliant.

'Oh, I go along with Lenny.' Bear made a tiny spreading gesture with the palms of his hands. 'Chief Superintendent Rucker's been lucky, but he's also done the right thing. That counts, too. If this John Doe character expects a police officer, I think Mr. Rucker should be the one if he's agreeable, of course. But if John Doe stipulates a "civilian" – and, if Lenny doesn't mind – I think Mr. Lennox should be on stand-by.'

'That's it, then.' Gilliant looked first at Sullivan, then at Sugden. 'Two and two . . . and I have the casting vote. It's your baby, Mr. Rucker.'

Rucker nodded his satisfaction.

Sullivan and Sugden frowned their disapproval for a moment, then cleared their minds of personal conflict and waited for Gilliant to lay down rules.

'We use wireless. Obviously,' said Gilliant. 'A hidden mike and transmitter with Mr. Rucker. No police cars. Nothing to frighten off the quarry. But well within wireless range. You, Mr. Sugden, Mr. Harris. And you, Mr. Lennox.'

'And me?' asked Sullivan.

'Of course. *And* Mr. Bear. I want Mr. Rucker straddled, right and left. With a team ahead of him and a team behind him at all times. Encircled, in fact. As he moves, and wherever he moves, the circle moves. A continuous talk-out by Mr. Rucker. Where he is, what he's doing and where his next destination is. Plain cars and vans. Walkie-talkie contact throughout. Nobody within sight, but none of the units more than half a mile from the change-over point, wherever it happens to be. That's the strategy, gentlemen. Hand-pick the men you require, then work out the details of the tactical side of things.'

Evening . . .

Bluff and counter-bluff. Or, if you will, stop and long-stop. The essence of all good police work; to be as sure as possible, but thereafter to accept the equal possibility of a mistake. The noose wherein the mysterious John Doe might shove his neck was plaited with care. The knot was examined and re-examined to ensure that it would tighten, and remain tight. But, parallel with all this, the normal murder enquiries continued without let-up.

The communication between John Doe and the police was kept from the media. The general public knew that a man-hunt was under way and they were satisfied.

A young man had been killed. The killer had to be found. The police were hell-bent on finding him. Who could ask for more?

Meanwhile it was Saturday evening.

*

The extra bar-staff reported for duty at the pubs. The disco-halls tested their garish lighting and their ear-splitting amplification systems. The strippers, the female impersonators and the blue-gag comedians opened their make-up boxes in the dressing rooms of the clubs and clip-joints.

It was Saturday evening.

In the county area, miles from Lessford or Bordfield, the men who worked the soil bathed the aches from their muscles and dressed in clothes which did not carry the faint stench of honest sweat. They close-shaved, brushed tractor-dirt from beneath their finger-nails and tried to comb some form of control into their unruly hair. They gathered in bar parlours of country inns, or in village halls, where local dances were being held. They were in the main slow-spoken men and shy, but their shyness, in some mysterious way, added something to their basic masculinity.

It was Saturday evening.

Turn the coin. Two parents mourned their son. A young girl mourned her lover. In the stillness of a silent complex geared to feed news to a local public an editor sat alone and blamed himself for something which was not his fault. Coppers continued to ask questions and continued to receive non-answers.

And, in a chapel of rest, the body of a murdered man lay within the silk lining of a newly-made coffin.

All these things, and more, but what the hell? It *was* Saturday evening.

SUNDAY – JULY 31st

I asked so little. To be left alone; having been born, to live and be a burden to no man and then to die. That was all I ever asked. I think no man has ever asked for less.

When Muriel died, I wept, and my tears came from a weight of inner pain which, at the time, I thought I could never carry. A pain which I thought would never ease. But in time it eased, it became bearable. Today it is a dull and opalescent sadness which encases a thousand happy memories. This too, I think, is part of death. Part of the death of the young Stephen Wrie; the hurt of those who knew him will pass and, in its place, there will be a strange happiness, built upon reminiscences.

A face will remind them. Or a tune, perhaps. Or a book he once read and enjoyed; a scene he once admired; the anniversary of some day which was an annual part of his life. A whole catalogue of reminders. And for a moment there will be a stab of agony but, after that, the memories will bring on the smiles.

They will never forgive. Civilisation, so-called, will ensure that they never forgive but, as the years pass, the hatred will cool. It will become a required mask but, behind the mask, there will be no real hatred.

This I know, from my own experience. Nobody loved more, or more completely, than I loved Muriel. Yet now, within three short years, I can remember, without pain.

I try to convey these facts of emotion to Kim.

I say, 'Sam was an unfortunate, my pet. The victim of circumstances.'

'He's in prison.'

The fury of youth is in that simple statement. A fury as blunt, as uncompromising, as the statement itself. I think I, too, experienced such fury when I was her age. It goes with the generation. Is part of life, before true age quietens the turmoil of pointless outrage.

I say, 'Prison. Some good men have spent part of their lives in prison. Men with principles.'

'Men who hit policemen with pick-handles.'

'Some,' I say, gently.

It does nothing to help. How can it? She was brought up – indeed, *I* brought her up – to respect the law. After her mother and myself, the uniformed policeman (*any* uniformed policeman) was the one man on God's earth she could trust. Completely. He was never a bogey-man, to be used as a threat when she misbehaved. He was always a friend; a good friend, and a man who stood, four-square, between herself and whatever evil she might encounter.

I taught her well, it would seem.

She picks a stray piece of cotton from the hem of her skirt and says, 'Sam. I thought he'd more sense. To get himself mixed up with the hooligan crowd.'

What can I say? What words of comfort can I give?

We have just returned from our normal attendance at the Communion Service. We have broken bread, we have sipped wine, we have joined others in the weekly commemoration of The Last Supper. If this means nothing, what words can I say?

She says, 'When I visit him. Pop, the other women . . . you wouldn't believe. I feel ashamed. Dirty.'

'They go for the same reason you go,' I remind her.

'I know.' Her voice is laden with disgust. 'For the same reason. To see a criminal. Some prisoner, no better than this "John Doe" who killed that poor young man on Friday. No better than him, and Sam's one of them.'

'We're – we're told to forgive,' I say, gently.

'Of course.' Her look carries mild surprise. 'Sam knows that. He's a good man. Weak. I think he's proved himself to be a weak man. But he mustn't do it again. He knows that. If he's no better than a bar-room brawler, I want no . . .'

'He's no bar-room brawler, pet,' I say. 'What he did, he did for our sake. For my sake. Because wicked men wrecked the firm. That's why.'

'Is violence an answer? To anything?'

I realise something. Suddenly and with a sense of shock. This daughter of mine is a grown woman, with a mind of her own and opinions of her own. She no longer takes what I say as the automatic truth. She questions. And when she doesn't agree, she fights back.

She is now fighting back.

She says, 'One day the fools who advocate violence will be met by a whole army of non-violence. A wall of decency. Then, who knows? They might even feel shame.'

'Violence has its place in the scheme of things,' I argue.

'I think not.'

'Render unto Caesar . . . And if Caesar's coin is the coin of violence, what then?'

Soon she will leave, to return to the neat little semi which she and Sam share on the other side of Lessford. It is a weekly routine; a pattern of Sunday morning life we have adopted since Sam was sent to prison. She never stays for lunch. Partly because I eat all my main meals out, and have done since the death of Muriel, and partly, I suspect, as a self-imposed penance on her part. At a guess prison is a very lonely place and, if Sam is lonely she, too, must be lonely. I know my daughter well. I know the way she thinks; the tracks upon which her own peculiar conscience must always run. She will eat alone. As much as possible, she will live alone. Once each week she will join me in prayer. Beyond that Sam's sentence is also Kim's sentence.

Strange principles, unless you have known and loved and lived with her mother. Muriel's principles were of a similar nature and one of the reasons for my love.

But soon she will leave and I have things to tell her.

I start by saying, 'This house. It's too big for one person.'

She hesitates, then tentatively suggests, 'A housekeeper?'

'A very ambiguous term,' I smile. 'You've sense enough to know I'd never marry again. Equally I couldn't share my bed with another woman.'

'I wasn't suggesting . . .'

'No housekeeper,' I say, firmly. I walk to the tiny roll-topped desk, push back the lid and pick up the fat, foolscap-sized envelope. I drop it on to the table and say, 'Yours, my pet.'

'What?' She frowns at the envelope.

'The house. This house. The deeds. The title is there . . . all it requires is your signature. All the legalities have been dealt with. Sign it, have it witnessed, then . . .'

'This house?'

'And the contents.'

'For heaven's sake, we already have . . .'

'I know.' I nod. 'And when he comes out he'll have to live there. The neighbours. The gossip. His sentence will never end, until you move house.'

'But – but we *couldn't* . . .'

'Kim, my pet.' I place my hands on her shoulders. 'Eventually, it will *be* yours. As a going concern if you take it now. Or as a derelict shell, filled with cobwebs and rotting furniture, if you wait until I join your mother. I'm leaving.'

'Leaving?'

'The house. The district. The country.'

'Where? Where are you going? And when? And why? For heaven's sake, why?'

'When? . . . Today. Tomorrow, at the latest. Where? . . . I haven't yet made up my mind. To Canada, I think. I have a notion that Canada might still have use for a skilled workman. Even though he is middle-aged. As for why? Because I need independence. Freedom. Something I haven't had since the firm folded. I need it, Kim. God, you don't know *how* I need it. I've tasted it, that's my trouble. Had I never tasted it, I might not have felt as I feel now. But now . . . I can't live without it. Ask Sam, my pet. Ask him and believe his answer. He knows. It's why he isn't with us. Ask him, believe him, and tell him I'll send for you both when I've found the place we're both looking for. Meanwhile – the house . . . don't be stiff-necked. Sign the transference papers and have it ready for him when he comes home.'

For ten, perhaps fifteen, minutes she argues. She argues well, and she argues passionately and, were I not a man with a mind of his own, it might have been more diffi-cult. But the child she once was is still on my side, and the child she once was would never have argued with her father. Therefore, she agrees. She weeps a little, then we kiss, then she leaves and I am free to concentrate upon the business of the day.

I study my map. It is, by the yardstick of any competent map-drawer, a poor thing. It is not to scale and it leaves out many streets, many side-roads and many cul-de-sacs. It concentrates on bare essentials.

The Rigfield Road area, on the outskirts of North End; where Rigfield Road underpasses a junction of the railway line, as that line leaves Lessford railway station.

There is a stretch of that road, two hundred yards perhaps, not much less, which passes under the viaducts. A gloomy, ill-lit two hundred yards along a road which arrows its way through the warehouse district of the city. Few people live there and Sunday is a particularly 'dead' day. I know the district well from the days when the firm was a successful concern. I know, for example, that there is a telephone kiosk at the junction with Rigfield Terrace and another kiosk at the junction with Rigfield

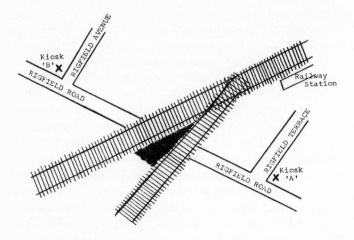

Avenue and, that to get from one kiosk to the other, it is necessary to go along Rigfield Road and under that two hundred yards of gloom. I also know that there is an 'unofficial' path which climbs the embankment at the junction of the two lines at the Rigfield Terrace side, a path used by linesmen working on the tracks, a short cut which some take rather than trudging the few hundred yards to the station. This and the station are my 'escape route'. Up the path, along the line and on to the platform. A train leaves for Preston at 12.38 p.m. It starts from Lessford, therefore there is no likelihood of it being late.

Plans, I think, should be simple. As uncomplicated as possible. They should be finalised and thereafter adhered to. Certain precautions should be taken, of course, and those precautions I have already dealt with. This morning at about 2 a.m. I visited the area. I checked the telephones. In each kiosk I dialled my home number and each time I heard the ringing tone. The kiosks have not been vandalized; the telephones are in working order. The tunnel – the long viaduct, under which the road passes – might have been purpose built. Yesterday evening after having telephoned the police, I walked through this tunnel. I carried a transistor radio, with its aerial fully extended and with it fine-tuned to Radio Four. The volume was at full blast and the batteries were new. Nothing! Within three yards of entering the tunnel, all reception had disappeared. It is, I think, the most perfect 'blind spot' as far as radio reception, and presumably radio transmission, is concerned for miles around.

Because one must, of course, face facts.

The police will bring the money. If I suggested otherwise, the courier would *still* be a policeman. Therefore why suggest otherwise? A police officer by all means. And, if a police officer, then he will be linked with other police officers, and how else other than by radio?

His colleagues will be out of sight. Of course they will . . . their purpose is to capture me, not scare me away.

There must, therefore, be a distance and, until I am identified, the meshes of the net must be wide enough to allow me entry. And without radio communication those same meshes will remain wide enough for me to make my escape.

Noon

I dial the number. The voice answers immediately. The same voice, the voice I have come to associate with the name 'Rucker'. An evil voice. A reptilian voice.

The voice says, 'Rucker here.'

'The money?' I ask.

'We have it.'

I must tread carefully. This conversation is no doubt being recorded. Already Post Office engineers will be testing circuits in an attempt to trace this call. Thank God for S.T.D., but my safety has very fixed limits.

I say, 'Unmarked notes?'

'What you asked for. But . . .'

'Just listen,' I interrupt. I say, 'The telephone kiosk at the junction of Rigfield Terrace and Rigfield Road. Be there in twenty minutes.'

'If you seriously think I'm going to . . .'

I replace my receiver.

I find I am sweating a little. The palms of my hands are moist. Perhaps I am a little afraid. If so I have cause to be. I am fighting for my life. For my future. For the future of Kim and Sam. I have a lot to lose. A lot? I have *everything* to lose. There must therefore be no mistakes.

I am not ashamed of my perspiration.

12.05 p.m.

I drive towards North End. Moderately. Not too fast, not too slowly and with almost exaggerated care. There is a certain excitement building up inside me, a breathlessness, but an excitement I would not wish to happen too often. A little like stage fright, perhaps? No, I think not, rather more like the fear of the unknown which enters the brain on the eve of a surgical operation. Everything is going to be all right, but *something* might go wrong. That sort of excitement. That sort of fear.

Alongside me, hidden under a car rug on the front

seat, is the gun. Fitted, oiled, loaded and ready for use. A silent companion. An inanimate object, but nevertheless a companion.

I find I have time in which to think. My thoughts revolve around Kim and they are thoughts which bring on a certain unease.

What she said, earlier this day. Her attitudes and her opinions. When she said, '. . . no better than this "John Doe" who killed that poor young man . . .' The disgust which mingled with her love for Sam. The overall and unqualified loathing she seems to have for all violence.

Strange.

She of all people should understand. This is not a killing spree. I get no enjoyment, no sense of achievement, in the taking of human life. But the rules demand it, the rules of a modern economic jungle. And the number one rule is brainless violence. Nor did I invent that rule, nor even subscribe to it before it was used upon me. It was the invention of evil, power-hungry men who lead an army of muddle-headed fools. The army grows and the leaders become more destructive. Eventually, and soon, they will take over. They will deny decency and out-scream democracy and on that day it will be too late. On that day there will be no escape. The law will become the law of the pig-pen. The madness will be complete and personal pride, personal achievement, will be out-lawed forever.

And yet my Kim does not appreciate this simple truth. She was suckled on a way of life which insists that mere power itself does not of necessity command respect. She was taught to mistrust power; to view it as megalomania until it had proved itself to be other. To fight it. To fight it to the very end with no holds barred.

She was taught these things, but it would seem she has forgotten them. Her attitude this morning was a negation of everything she has been taught to believe in.

Which means she wouldn't understand.

This that I'm doing, this last desperate charge towards some degree of sanity, is, it would seem, something which might even shock her. The realisation saddens me, but I must accept it as a fact. I must alter my plans accordingly.

Certain it is that I must give careful thought to my original scheme for sending for Kim and Sam if and when I am settled at my final destination. They will know where I am, only if I am one-hundred-per-cent sure that that knowledge will not be misused; that it will not be passed on to the police.

No, my pet, my beloved Kim, you have, I fear, seen the last of me, pending certain proof that this morning's outburst was a mere whimsical back-tracking upon what you have been taught to believe. A temporary spat of womanly perversity.

Otherwise . . .

12.15 p.m.

I park the car.

I park it in North End. On a street with no sides; a street with no name; a street which forms a littered lane between areas of rubble-strewn debris. Where rows of stinking terrace houses have been bulldozed to the ground in a mad landscape of demolished bricks and levelled walls.

I can prophesy what will happen to my car.

I know my North End and know that the scavengers will already be watching. Even as I close the door and walk away from the vehicle they will be smiling their anticipatory glee. Before the afternoon is out the wheels will have gone. And the battery and tool kit. And perhaps the seats and registration plates. By morning the engine will have been removed, and tomorrow, or probably the next day, the younger element of this rag-bag of humanity will have fixed up some makeshift fuse to the almost-empty petrol tank and the end will be an explosion, followed by a blaze which will effectively destroy all identification.

Within a week even the twisted metal will have been sold to some back-street scrap merchant.

Theft and vandalism can have their uses.

12.17 p.m.

I am, I know, within the net. Don't ask me *how* I know. Don't ask me to explain the tingling at the nape of my neck. That I am somewhere within the unseen police cordon is something which a sixth sense screams at me.

Understand me. I can see nothing: no strangely parked cars or vans; no dawdling stranger, busy doing nothing in particular. Wherever they are, they are out of sight and if I cannot see *them* they, I hope, cannot see *me*. Nevertheless, they are there. I know!

I use the back streets as much as possible; a zig-zag course which will bring me to Rigfield Road, north of the junction with Rigfield Avenue. The stench disgusts me the canyons between the series of high-rise blocks trap the stink of this foul place. Most of the ground floor windows are smashed and not a few of the first floor windows. The other windows rise, in tiers, to the sky and gaze down at me like sightless eyes. But not *so* sightless, of that I am sure. I am being watched. My progress is being logged. Not by police, the inhabitants of this area would never allow their hovels to be used as a watching post by their enemies, but by creatures who are for ever suspicious of strangers. The 'North Enders'. The hooligans of this city; the madmen and the equally mad women, whose irrational hatred of all creatures other than themselves is a mutagenic by-product of this present age of indiscriminate destruction.

I walk briskly. I must not be late. Rucker, I have no doubt, is already waiting at the Rigfield Terrace kiosk. Waiting for instructions. Waiting with the money with which I can buy my way out of this crazy, illogical community.

I am wearing an unbelted mac. Unbuttoned, but because my hands are in its pockets, kept closed. Under the mac, the shoulder-plate resting at the bottom of the right 'poacher's pocket', is my rifle. Hidden, but ready. Loaded and needing only pressure on the trigger to send its bullet in any direction I choose.

12.20 p.m.

The pips come over the wire and I press the coin into its slot and say, 'Rucker?'

'Who else?' His voice is almost bored.

'You have some walking to do,' I say.

'If you think I'm going to spend the day . . .'

'Walk,' I say in a hard voice. 'I want no motorcade. Bit at a time. We'll meet eventually.'

There is a pause, then he says, 'I'm listening.'

'Go to the kiosk at the junction of Rigfield Road and Rigfield Avenue.'

'What the hell? That's only . . .'

'Bit at a time,' I repeat. 'Be there in fifteen minutes. I'll be in touch.'

I replace the receiver and leave the kiosk, the kiosk I have just instructed him to come to.

Cunning, you see, must be met by cunning. Even the words must be carefully weighed. '*Go* to the kiosk', not '*Come* to the kiosk'. By implication, it suggests that he is moving away from me when in fact he is walking towards me. And walking. I need him to walk. And the bit about meeting 'eventually'. More cunning. I have planted in his mind the conviction that his day is to be taken up by moving from telephone kiosk to telephone kiosk. I have grafted a sense of monotony on to this exercise. It will unguard him and make things very much easier.

I walk along Rigfield Road towards the viaducts.

12.26 p.m.

And here he is.

We are less than ten yards from each other. He walks north, I walk south and we share the same pavement. Our footsteps echo in the deserted cavern which is the viaduct carrying the railway tracks above our heads. I have met nobody. I have seen no vehicle and the slight curve of the road hides us from the rest of the world.

In that little more than a second I see the man who so easily plays at being contemptuous. A thin man; a gaunt man, with an easy, long-striding pace. An arrogant man; the manner in which he holds himself, the easy way in which he swings the leather Gladstone bag, smacks of arrogance.

His arrogance has little time left in which to live.

As we draw abreast, I say, 'Rucker?'

He stops suddenly. He turns to face me and the contempt on his face eliminates any last doubt.

He opens his mouth to speak, but he does not speak.

I already have my finger on the trigger and my left hand is across my body, under my mac, and tilting the snout of the silencer into line with his throat. I squeeze the trigger and the noise is a little like a heavy book being dropped on to a padded surface, not at all like a rifle shot. And, anyway, if he *is* carrying a microphone, it matters not at all. I have already verified that the walled-in and roofed viaduct forms the perfect 'blind spot' as far as radio reception and transmission are concerned.

Before he can speak, he has no face. The bullet takes him under the chin, cleaves a way up and through the top of his skull and presumably buries itself in the black brickwork of the arch. The impact lifts him from his feet, turns him and smashes him against the dank wall.

He is dead. Of course he is dead. I could not possibly allow a police officer to see my face, and live.

12.28 p.m.

And for nothing, for *nothing*!

The thin chain, linking the handle of the Gladstone bag to the steel bracelet which circles his wrist. And the bag itself; thick, seasoned leather, stitched and riveted, and with a lock which I could never force.

And inside that bag? God knows. Perhaps the money. Perhaps not. Perhaps nothing, the imaginary crock of gold at the end of my own impossible rainbow.

I go a little mad.

I turn the dead thing on to its back, lift the bag on to its chest, then kneel and try to force open the tight-locked top with my bare hands. I think I mouth an endless stream of whispered obscenities as I struggle. Then my right hand slips, plunges itself palm-first into the scarlet curd that was once a face, and sanity returns with a rush.

Real sanity. Complete sanity. A sanity which accuses me of everything I have done. Of this. Of the murder of Stephen Wrie. Of the measureless misery I must have caused. Of the brutal theft I have so carefully worked out and almost accomplished.

I have difficulty in pushing myself upright. I leave great crimson daub-marks on the wall. My legs tremble and at first have difficulty in not folding up beneath me, but I gulp in air, fight the shaking muscles and force myself to move. To walk. Then to run. And as I run I strip myself of the bloodstained mac and throw it and that damned home-made rifle on to the pavement behind me.

12.32 p.m.

They say madness gives strength and fear gives wings.

How true, how true.

I can hardly remember scrambling up the embankment. I noticed nothing; police cars – a whole cordon of uniformed officers – and I wouldn't have even seen them. But now I am racing alongside the sleepers and ahead of me I can see the first incline of a platform.

Some tiny grain of self-preservation drives me forward. To the platform. Past the trolleys. Towards the waiting train.

That same pinpoint of self-preservation makes me do the right things. Despite the panic. Despite the sickening horror. Despite the utter self-disgust.

I slow to a walk as I reach the busier part of the station. I find the train, open a second class door then immediately open the facing toilet, lock the door and hold my head over the washbowl as all the fear and all the disgust and all the self-hatred bursts out in a single stream of vomit.

I am still hawking and trying to pump something from an empty stomach as the train leaves the station.

SUNDAY – JULY 31st

12.15 p.m.

One behind, one ahead, one to his right, one to his left.
A Vauxhall, a Ford, an Austin pickup and a Morris van;
all police vehicles, but not one of which looked like a
police vehicle. They formed the inner circle around
Rucker and the small fortune which Rucker carried
chained to his wrist. Beyond them and forming an outer
circle were the squad cars; some parked, some cruising
within a limited and determined area. Men on foot filled
what few gaps were left; two C.I.D. men at the station
entrance, two more at the bus depot. The taxi stands,
too, were covered.

Rucker was safe. Wherever he moved – wherever the
killer placed him – the ring of law-enforcement would
follow.

And yet . . .

Sullivan was on edge. Every few moments he took a
deeper-than-usual breath; a miniature sigh. His eyes were
never still. He sat hunched forward in the front passenger seat of the Vauxhall, and his tension could be felt
by the driver and the two plain clothes men in the back
seat.

He held the microphone in his right hand and, for the
umpteenth time, he checked that the other three vehicles
were in position.

To the Ford. 'Big Daddy to Number One. Come in,
please.'

Bear's voice came back, over the speaker. 'Number One to Big Daddy. Go ahead.'

'Anything?'

'Not a sausage, Dick. We're in position at the round-about. We have every car that's turned into Rigfield Road. Other than that we're ready for your say-so.'

'Fine. Keep your eyes skinned. Rucker left us, four minutes back, he should be at the kiosk by now.' Sullivan paused, then continued, 'Big Daddy to Number Two.'

'We heard it.' Sugden's voice came back from the Austin pickup. 'We're in the station forecourt. And ready.'

'Thanks. Number Three, come in.'

From the Morris van Harris's voice said, 'No slip-ups here. We're in position at the car park.'

'Good.' Sullivan moistened his lips, and repeated, 'Good. Be ready to move the minute we know which direction.'

He released the transmit button and stared ahead through the windscreen. Something was wrong, dammit, something was *wrong*! This bastard John Doe was nobody's fool. No thump-'em-and-scare-'em wallah. This one had grey matter. He'd *know*. He'd know damn well there'd be a trap. A trap of some sort. Damnation, he'd even asked a copper to deliver the loot. A copper, for Christ's sake. Because he knew, he had sense enough to know, that who the hell did the actual hand-over, the fuzz had to be within whistling distance.

Ruthlessness and brains. It was one hell of a combination.

Rucker's voice came through the speaker.

'Here he is. The phone's ringing. Hold your water, gentlemen. I'll be back with you when the lunatic's said what he has to say.'

Rucker's voice said, 'Well, now we know. The idiot must have shares in a shoe firm.'

'Rucker!' Sullivan spat the word into the microphone. 'Cut the heroics. We want to know.'

'The Rigfield Avenue kiosk.'

'For Christ's sake . . .'

'I know. You can damn near see it from here.' Rucker's sardonic chuckle came over the air. 'And will I please walk. Fifteen minutes from now he'll ring me at the Rigfield Avenue box. This gets more like Snakes and Ladders by the minute.'

'Keep in touch,' said Sullivan, harshly.

'But of course.'

Sullivan took a deep breath, then said, 'Big Daddy to One, Two and Three. Stay where you are. He's still ringed. This is going to be cat-and-mouse stuff. Stay where you are until we know which way to move.'

Sullivan shouted into the microphone.

'Rucker! Rucker! Come in, Rucker. Where the hell are you?'

There was a moment of silence, then Bear's voice said, 'He hasn't come this way.'

'Nor this,' said Sugden's voice.

'Nor this,' repeated the voice of Harris.

Sullivan said, 'Okay, One, Two and Three. Stay put. We're going to risk it. We're going to cruise past the Rigfield Avenue kiosk.'

The driver of the Vauxhall didn't wait to be told. He

slipped the stick into first, then second, turned right along Rigfield Road and at a steady twenty-five cruised towards the viaducts.

They found Rucker. That it *was* Rucker could be seen by the Gladstone bag, still chained to his wrist. Other than that identification was impossible. Who the hell can identify a man whose front half of his head is missing?

And a train gradually gathered speed on its journey from Lessford to Preston.

3 p.m.

So many things happened at or about that third hour after noon on that damp and miserable Sunday in July. So many things. They added up to anger and disgust, heartbreak and helplessness, shock and (yes, even) a stirring of ambition, plus something else.

That extra something?

Sullivan caught a hint of it as he addressed a crowded Operations-Centre-cum-Recreation-Room. A genuinely crowded room this time, not merely an assemblage of top-rankers. This time the audience included inspectors, sergeants, not a few detective constables and a handful of uniformed beat men. All the chairs were occupied and more men and women stood than sat. It was as if the whole force, the complete M.P.D., was present by proxy, if not in person.

Sullivan stood there and punched home a message they all knew by heart. Bear and Harris flanked him, seated and grim-faced. Like flying buttresses, silently augmenting the granite-hard tone of the deputy chief constable's voice.

Sullivan was saying, '. . . We'll pin the photographs up on the notice board. Then you can see. They'll make you puke, but that doesn't matter a damn, as long as you remember that what you're looking at was once Detective Chief Superintendent Rucker. One of your colleagues. It'll help you. It'll make you *realise*.

'We have the gun. We have the raincoat. We've something to go on. We know where the bastard was at a certain time. What the hell else, he's not invisible. Somebody must have seen him. *Must* have seen him. He bought the raincoat. It didn't just materialise, he bought it. Or maybe had it given. Or maybe nicked it from somewhere. But that's a link. One link. The other link's the gun. Forensic have it at the moment, but it'll be here the minute they've finished with it. It has dabs on it. Dabs all over it. But forget 'em. We've checked and double-checked. Those dabs aren't on police files. We haven't had him before. It helps. It means we can forget the comedians we *have* had. All the germs we *have* fingerprinted. They're out. The man we're looking for has no previous record.

'No previous record. But he hates the police and, if you doubt that, you'll change your mind when you see those photographs.'

Sullivan paused, took a deep breath then, in a tone a shade lower than before, he continued, 'It has to be said. Detective Chief Superintendent Rucker didn't head the popularity poll. Some of you – a lot of you – didn't like him too much. Forget it! He was a copper. One of us, one of you. Just remember this. If you – any one of you – were there on that slab, where he is, you'd want the bastard caught. You'd want it. You'd expect it. And, if mortally possible, you'd *get* it. If I find one man, one woman, who doesn't subscribe to that theory and one-hundred-per-cent, that man, that woman, won't know what the hell's hit 'em. Rucker was a police officer. And nobody – *nobody* – kills a police officer and still walks the streets.'

*

Gilliant himself broke the news. And with Gilliant was Rucker's immediate superior, Sugden. And a police-woman sergeant. Rank ⤳ the rank of detective chief superintendent – carried that brand of prestige.

Nor was there an easy way.

There never is. Ask any copper, he'll tell you. You can use the indirect method; you can root out some relative, break the news to him or her, and then leave it to the relative to tell the next-of-kin. It's a coward's way, because you've still got to be there when the wall col-lapses, when the next-of-kin takes it right in the teeth. You'll still be there, as helpless as ever and, for a bonus, you'll know you ducked a particularly lousy job. You can go in with a smile, not a happy smile, but a smile which carries genuine sympathy and friendship. But the smile won't last long. No smile on God's earth is going to blunt the blade of truth when you drive it home.

Gilliant did it the quick way, because there was no easy way.

Rucker's wife took it, stone-faced and without a tremor. She nodded, once, then seemed to wait, patiently, for details.

The policewoman sergeant stepped forward and murmured, 'I should sit down, Mrs. Rucker.'

'Why?' Rucker's wife looked genuinely puzzled at the suggestion.

Sugden said, 'Sit down, Mrs. Rucker. Please.'

It might have been a shrug, indeed it might have been a tiny shrug of resignation, but whatever it was it was followed by a quick, tight smile, and she lowered herself into an armchair.

She said, 'I could – er . . . I could use a cigarette.'

Gilliant was as near a non-smoker as to make no dif-ference. Sugden was a pipe man. They both glanced at the policewoman sergeant and she took a packet of Gold

Leaf from her tunic pocket, opened it and, when Rucker's wife had selected a cigarette, flicked a lighter into flame and held it for this woman who had suddenly become a widow.

'He was . . .' Gilliant cleared his throat. 'He was doing his duty, Mrs. Rucker. He was taking a calculated risk. I know it's small comfort, but . . .'

'It's no comfort at all, Mr. Gilliant,' she interrupted. 'He's dead. The manner of his death may be of some interest to the honour – so-called – of the police service. It matters not at all to me.'

'I'm sorry,' said Gilliant gently.

'I'm not.' She blew a stream of smoke as she spoke. 'I'm not sorry. I'm not glad. The truth is, I'm not particularly interested.'

In a low, shocked voice, Sugden breathed, 'Good God!'

'Did you expect me to faint, Mr. Sugden?' The quick, tight smile came and went. It might have been Rucker himself talking as she added, 'My apologies, if I've disappointed you.'

'You're – you're his *wife*!' Indignation jostled with disgust in the policewoman sergeant's tone.

'Which means?' She raised slightly sardonic eyebrows.

'You – you love him . . . or, at least, loved him. Once.'

'Did I? I often wonder.' She inhaled cigarette smoke, then said, 'Is it possible, do you think? For anybody to love a man like that? To love so hateful a person? Is it possible? *Ever* possible?'

Gilliant made as if to speak, but held back the words as he saw her face. Her expression remained as rock-firm as ever. No sorrow. No sadness. And her voice was as steady, as unemotional as ever. The tears spilled from the out-of-focus eyes and streamed down her cheeks, but she seemed unaware of them. She continued to smoke the cigarette. Calmly. Unhurriedly. It was as if the heartbreak was buried deep inside; locked there by layers of loathing and yet there. Able to escape only through the eyes, as liquid misery which the rest of her mind and body refused to acknowledge.

She said, 'His work. His profession. He hated it, like he hated everything else. Everybody else. He could see good in nothing and nobody. There was – there was something wrong with him. Something terribly wrong. A terrible illness. He never laughed. No, that's wrong, he laughed. But at the wrong things. Where normal men would have had some compassion. Where they'd have felt pity. He laughed. That's when he laughed. At other people's misfortune. He laughed then. A mocking laughter.' She paused, then in a softer, more hateful tone, she continued, 'He laughed when I had the miscarriage. When I lost the child. He didn't want it, that's what he said, he didn't want a family. And he laughed then. And when they told me. No more babies. That was another time he laughed. He laughed and made some horrible remark about not having the smell of soiled nappies in the house. That was the sort of man he was. The sort of – of . . .'

Then she cracked. Slowly. Almost unwillingly. The layers broke away and she raised her head and gazed at Gilliant through tears she finally acknowledged. Her face crumpled and her voice dropped to little more than a whisper.

She said, 'Understand him, Mr. Gilliant. Mr. Sugden. Please. Try to understand him. He was the most unhappy man I ever knew. The most unhappy man alive. It was – it was . . . his way. He – he refused to be hurt. Refused! No matter what. The miscarriage . . . he refused to be hurt. When we couldn't – when I couldn't . . . he refused to be hurt. That was his illness. I know. I lived with him . . . I *know*. He could stand being loathed. He could stand being hated. He – he trained himself. Forced himself. *He couldn't stand being hurt.* It – it made him what he is . . . what he *was*.' And now the tears ran unchecked and the sobs threatened to choke her as she said, 'Love him a little . . . please! His name. His memory. Love him . . . just a little. *I* loved him. We fought. We hated each other, truly hated each other . . . but I still loved him. Because I knew. This weakness. This silly weakness. Not being hurt. It – it tortured him. Made him what he was. Now . . . Now, he's dead. Y-you can . . . We – we needn't hate him quite as much. Need we? We can – we can love him. Just a little . . . can't we? Please!'

Her head dropped and the sobs shook her whole body.

Gilliant murmured, 'Stay with her, sergeant.'

'Yes, sir.'

'Anything she wants. Anything we can do. Don't hesitate.'

'Yes, sir. I'll see to things.'

As the two men walked down the drive towards the waiting car Sugden growled, 'The poor bastard.'

'Him? Or, her?'

'Both of 'em.'

Gilliant said, 'A hell of a life.'

Monday morning's edition of *The Lessford and Bordfield Tribune* was being planned. The editorial conference was under way, the six-times-a-week gathering of the deputy editor, the sub-editors and the features editor, under the chairmanship of Walter Kingsley. And Kingsley looked like a man on the verge of collapse. Ashen-faced. Red-eyed from lack of sleep. Wild-haired and unshaven. He chain-smoked cigarettes as he demanded the near-impossible from his aides.

'The whole paper,' he insisted. 'Every page. Every angle. I don't give a damn if World War Three breaks out between now and when the presses roll. That's the only thing we cover. We owe them that.'

'Look, chief . . .' One of the subs moved his hands in exaggerated gestures of helplessness. 'We can't do it. Front page, okay. A feature, maybe. The editorial. But after that? There's a limit, chief.'

'This,' rasped Kingsley, 'is one time when we are not going to "discuss". I'm not asking. I'm not suggesting. I'm ordering.'

The sports editor said, 'I can't see what the sports page can . . .'

'There'll *be* no sports page.'

'The hell! The whole balance goes to blazes without . . .'

'No sports page!' Kingsley stared – glared – at the assembly of men and women responsible for the production of the newspaper. His voice was almost a snarl of frustration. 'Will you people get this thing clear. Wrie. Now Rucker. This newspaper's responsible. *I'm* responsible. We're not going to forget that. And none of our readers is going to forget that. They're not going to be allowed to forget it. Two murders in three days, because *we* ignored a letter. That's our track record, ladies and gentlemen. We can't duck it and we're not going to try to duck it. Call it hair-shirt journalism if you like. Call it any name you fancy. But if it's possible to make amends we're going to make amends in tomorrow's edition. All I want from you today is suggestions. Not what gets published. Only *how* it gets published.'

One of the women present moistened her lips and said, 'The women's page . . .'

'Wrie had a mother and a girl friend. Rucker had a wife. Every policeman has a mother or a wife or a girl friend or a daughter. For God's sake, women are *there*. Behind the two men who were murdered. Behind every police officer in the force. Punch that simple fact home.

142

Take two pages, three if necessary. But make the break-fast-reading public aware. Make them understand.'

'Make them cry in their corn-flakes,' murmured the features editor, sarcastically.

'From *you*,' snapped Kingsley, 'I want something Swaffer might not have been ashamed of. Simple facts, simply told. Forget the pseudo-Hemingway style. It's beyond your capabilities.'

'Such praise.'

'Just try to put yourself in Rucker's shoes. On the point of having half your head shot away. As part of your job and for a pittance. And the various columnists. The freelancers. When you leave here contact them. I want as many as *them* in on this thing, too. Deadline, ten o'clock tonight. Tell them to phone their copy in, and warn the telephonists to be ready and waiting. What they think about it. Why *they* aren't police officers.' He turned to the news editor. 'You, Jim, get the reporters out. Interviews. From policemen. From Chief Constable Gilliant down. Facts, opinions and quotes. Every man on this one line. The man-in-the-street, the hooligans, the do-gooders. Everybody. Drain it dry. It's the only story we're going to run.'

As Kingsley chain-lit another cigarette, the art editor said, 'I don't see what . . .'

'I do.' Kingsley squashed the smoked cigarette into an ash-tray. 'Photographs. Photographs *Picture Post* wouldn't have turned down. The scenes of the crimes. Pictures of the victims, and *good* pictures. Reconstructions. Dig into the files. Find out what interests Wrie and Rucker had. Music. Reading. The cinema. Which television programmes they liked. What their hobbies were. Then pieces about those hobbies and interests.' He paused, looked at his team in silence for a moment, then ended, 'I want them to live. Those two men we indirectly killed. I want to grant them one more day of life. Not as cardboard characters, but as complete individuals. I want everybody who buys tomorrow's *Tribune* to *know* them. Tomorrow's copy belongs to them. Exclusively. That way . . .' He took a deep breath, then said, 'That way they might not be forgotten.'

It was the end of the conference. A unique conference, as far as every man and woman present was concerned. A conference they'd remember for the rest of their lives. They rose to their feet and made their ways towards the door.

Kingsley spoke to the deputy editor.

He said, 'Before you go, Mat.'

The deputy editor nodded and returned to his chair. He was an elderly man, older than Kingsley and with many years of journalism behind him. A kindly man. A man unsoured by a profession renowned for its percentage of cynics. He'd been deputy editor for a long time, he'd guided Kingsley and three of Kingsley's predecessors through their first few months of editorship. His days of ambition were long past. He was content to be what he was, the steadying influence behind a good newspaper and as near indispensable as any man could hope to be.

When they were alone Kingsley said, 'The editorial, Mat. I'll leave that to you. You know what I want. No purple passages. No heart-throb stuff. But something to make 'em sit up and take notice. You can do it a thousand times better than me.'

The deputy editor nodded.

Kingsley said, 'And the rest. As a favour. *You* check it, every word. I'll give it a re-check, but you check it first. I'm too close. Too involved. Just, y'know, give them both what they deserve. What the *Tribune* owes to them.'

He didn't know it and, had he known it, he wouldn't have cared, but Kingsley was launching newspaper history. The next issue of *The Lessford and Bordfield Tribune* was due to become a collector's item.

*

For a few days, then, starting that last Sunday in July, Lessford became known as 'the murder town'. The name was first coined locally, then the more lurid of the nationals caught the name and recognised it as a booster for sales. The television networks grabbed a piece of the action and, in a few million households, po-faced newscasters fed the latest international flapdoodle to a square-eyed public, moved on to the newest industrial shunt-up, then went into an inter-round summary concerning the goings on at Lessford, 'the murder town'.

Detective Chief Superintendent Rucker became something of a national hero. In life he'd been a pain in the neck, in death he symbolised 'the thin blue line' between anarchy and law and order.

Odd, little mention was made of Stephen Wrie.

Richard Wrie listened to the on-the-hour news bulletins on the radio and muttered, 'What about *our* lad? He's just as dead. T' same booger did 'em both in. So, what about *our* lad?'

Not that he wanted sympathy. Or even notoriety. He merely wanted recognition of his murdered son; an understanding that Rucker hadn't been the first; a reminder that whereas, with Rucker, there had been some sort of reason – some sort of logical motive – with Wrie, it had been senseless and utterly meaningless slaughter.

But, you see, Wrie hadn't been a copper.

Rucker had. And a copper with much weight of rank across his narrow shoulders.

You want to hit the headlines? You want to see a police force go coldly berserk? You want to see the whole might of a law-machine aimed right at *you*? Go ahead, kill a copper : then find the nearest dark corner and cringe there for the rest of your miserable life.

The argument goes thus :

Kill a copper and you'll stop at nothing. Kill a copper and the ancient rite of outlawry is resurrected. You have no friends, because no man can afford to *be* your friend. The legend tells it all. 'No man, woman or child has *ever* killed a copper and not been brought to justice.' Browne and Kennedy almost pulled it off, on the morning of September 27th, 1927; they gunned down Police Constable Gutteridge of the Essex Constabulary and, for full measure, sent bullets through the dead copper's eyes . . . just to be on the safe side. No witnesses. No known motive. Nothing. Okay, it took a long time and a lot of lost sleep, but Browne was hanged at Pentonville and Kennedy was hanged at Wandsworth, and, no doubt, as they met at the mouth of Hell they remembered the legend. 'No man, woman or child has *ever* killed a copper, and not been brought to justice.'

That, also, was something that happened at or about the third hour after noon, on that damp and miserable Sunday in July. The memory was rekindled. The legend was remembered. And almost six thousand coppers silently swore that, this time, also . . .

6 p.m.

'I have the feeling.' Gilliant tapped the copy of the report from the Forensic Science Laboratory, on the table before him. 'This is going to be a long slog. Mostly uphill work. Let's not go bull-headed. Keep things in third gear, we'll get there easier.'

Sullivan and Sugden tasted their newly-pulled pints.

Sullivan said nothing.

Sugden lowered his glass, then said, 'That bracelet-and-chain gag. It was asking for trouble.'

'It was Rucker's own idea,' said Gilliant.

'Aye, and it got him killed.'

There was no real answer to that observation. That, strictly speaking, it wasn't true didn't matter, because that was something only the killer knew. The simple solution, the obvious solution, was that this John Doe character had blown Rucker's head apart because of pique. Because of frustration. Because, after all his ring-a-ding brainwork, he *still* hadn't been able to get his hands on the fifty thousand smackers.

Killers tend to think along those lines.

The six men – Gilliant, Sullivan, Bear, Sugden, Harris and Lennox – were seated at a corner table in the 'Officers' Club' in the basement of the Lessford M.P.D. Headquarters. In fact, it wasn't a 'club' in the strict sense of that word, it was the canteen for the use of police officers of the rank of superintendent and above. But it had a well-stocked bar and, on most evenings, a scattering of high-rankers could be found talking shop while they wet their slightly superior whistles around the strategically placed tables. And on a case as big as the Wrie – Rucker murder enquiry it was the perfect spot for semi-relaxation while, at the same time, being within calling distance of the Operations-Centre-cum-Recreation Room, should some sudden and unexpected break occur in the investigation.

Bear sipped bitter lemon, and said, 'He should have been armed.'

'Probably,' agreed Gilliant, 'but that smacks of being wise after the event.'

'Nevertheless, we knew this villain was a killer.'

'No-o.' Lennox shook his massive head. He, too, was drinking beer. He tasted, swallowed, then said, 'Wild West stuff, squire. It don't sit easy on the public conscience.'

'Trained marksmen,' contributed Harris.

'The mac.' Gilliant's finger continued to tap the triple-sheeted report on the table in front of him. 'One of the buy-one-anywhere makes. There's nothing to show where it was sold, much less who bought it. Carr and his boffins have given it the whole treatment. Dust from the pockets. Stains. The lot. It could be anybody's. Yours, mine, anybody's. The gun? The barrel's from a Weatherby, they *think.* If so, it's been shortened and re-bored. The firing mechanism's from a Mauser and the chamber's from an adapted Lee-Enfield. The sight and mounting are standard. Leupold sight, Detacho mount. The rest is bits and pieces, but well made. *Very* well made. We're after a craftsman. A very skilled craftsman. And somebody with the equipment at hand to do the job. Fingerprints of course. All over the thing. They don't mean much. He hasn't been through police hands before.'

'He knows Lessford,' growled Sullivan. 'That bloody viaduct. It's one of the few radio blind spots in the city.'

'He knows Lessford,' agreed Gilliant. He sipped at his whisky and soda and added, 'The sight and the mounting. They're our best bet. Not many gunsmiths sell them. There should be a record.'

'Wise, though,' murmured Harris. Harris's drink was lager. He drank it sparingly, as if savouring the light brew on his tongue, before swallowing. 'Cunning,' he said. 'Five gets you ten he didn't buy that sight, or the mounting, within fifty miles of here.'

Gilliant said, 'It has a number. It can be traced.'

'Knowing gunsmiths . . .' Harris left the observation unfinished.

'All right.' Bear seemed to tire of the squirrel-cage conversation. 'Let's see what we've got. A man. He knows Lessford. Knows it well. Chances are he lives somewhere in Lessford. Somebody who can handle metal. A skilled fitter. Skilled mechanic. He can get hold of bits and pieces of various guns. That's not too easy . . .'

'But not too difficult,' interrupted Lennox. 'The damn

148

things are everywhere. All you have to do is look. Ask. They're around.'

'Service ammunition,' continued Bear.

'Lots of *that* around, too,' said Sullivan. 'Every Tom, Dick and Harry from the war has a souvenir round stuck at the back of a drawer somewhere.'

'But he'd have to ask.' Bear ploughed on, despite the attempts to dampen his summary. 'Guns. Three separate guns. He'd have to find them. Buy them. Something, even if they were only parts. And he's short of money. Desperately short of money. He's prepared to kill to get money, that's how desperate he is.'

'And *still* is.' Sugden's eyes narrowed slightly. 'That's an angle we mustn't forget. He's killed twice for damn-all. There's a chance. He might come again.'

'I dunno . . .' Lennox frowned, but his objection was only a token gesture.

Then there was a silence. These men were old hands at the game. They'd seen it all, heard it all, and were beyond surprise. They knew – or thought they knew – the criminal mind. The twisted logic of the murderer. The one-track cunning of the blackmailer.

And the built-in weakness of both species. The belief of such a man that he has usurped God; that the laws of man no longer apply and that he can plunge his way through such laws using his superior wit as a spearhead.

'It's possible,' mused Sullivan. 'More than possible.'

Gilliant nodded silent agreement.

Bear said, 'If he does, this time we go in armed.'

Lennox looked unhappy and grunted, 'He's lost his gun.'

'For God's sake, Lenny !'

'I'm for playing it safe and going in with revolvers,' said Harris.

Sugden said, 'Me, too. Damn it, he's killed twice. He

might have a whole armoury of do-it-yourself guns for all we know.'

'*If* he comes again,' said Gilliant, softly.

'It's possible,' said Sugden. 'Even probable. It's something we can't afford to overlook.'

'Mr. Sullivan.' Gilliant took up the reins of command. 'Your pigeon, I think. Three-man teams on permanent stand-by round the clock. Volunteers, if you can get them. A squad car at their immediate disposal. Pick them carefully. No medal-chasers. Responsible men, who've had recent range-training and who usually hit what they're aiming at. Three .45 magnums from the armoury, and ten rounds issue per man.'

MONDAY – AUGUST 1st to
THURSDAY – AUGUST 4th

The splinter incidents from the Wrie – Rucker killings flew, ricochetted and bounced off a score of different lives. Mere death is bad enough, but the manner of death of those who are murdered can reflect its violence upon the living. It can magnify the hurt to a point almost beyond tolerance. It can foster aggression, re-heat old hatreds and warp lives until they become twisted things, without hope or joy.

Murder is far more than the taking of life. It affects those within the orbit of its commission. It dredges the depths of tribal memory, slashes fissures in the top-surface of civilization and allows the animal passions of feud and ancient superstitions to ooze their way into daylight. It becomes the trigger for black thoughts, an evil which begets other evils and a vehicle upon which travel perverse irrationalities.

Sullivan suddenly found himself lumbered with 'wife trouble'. Not of the bedroom variety. Not of the spend-thrift brand. Not of the nagging type, at least not strictly speaking. But, nevertheless, 'wife trouble', in large dollops.

The truth was Mary Sullivan had had a basket-full. She'd been a good wife and a good copper's wife, which is not quite the same thing, for one hell of a long time. She tried to remember when, if ever, her life hadn't been dominated by that all-embracing phrase 'the exigencies of the service'. When decently cooked meals hadn't ended up as warmed-up mush. When evenings out hadn't had to be cancelled at the last minute. When they'd been able to ask friends in for an evening without the blasted phone ringing, calling this husband away from his duty as host. When, in fact, *anything* without the police force stepping in and screwing things up. Damn it, yes, more than once when they'd actually been making love. Even then!

And now, this.

'It's murder,' she stormed. 'All right, it's murder. But, God in heaven, you've handled murders before.'

Sullivan tried to explain. He pleaded. He said, 'It's not just the murders, pet. It's the issue of firearms. Armed policemen.'

'Guns. Big deal,' mocked Steve.

Steve was Sullivan's son, and Steve had attained the status of young adulthood. Steve, moreover, was a man, therefore Sullivan felt himself to be on firmer ground.

He snarled, 'Who the hell asked *you*?'

'Who the hell ever asks anybody?' parried Steve. 'In this house? In this house, the big bwana unzips and we all speak in whispers.'

Sullivan was not the first father to make that particularly brainless remark, 'If I were twenty years younger . . .'

'If you were twenty years younger,' said Steve, solemnly, 'you wouldn't be my father and, moreover, I'd take you apart and *make* you see sense.'

'I can still . . .'

'You *can't*! Hell's bells, can't you see? That's what we're both getting at. You no longer *can*. Ease it, man. Cool it. Act your age for a change.'

'Stop it!' Mary Sullivan ran her fingers through her hair, then in a calmer voice said, 'Stop it, the pair of you.' She lowered herself on to one of the kitchen chairs, looked directly into Sullivan's face and said, 'All right. Let's assume I understand. I've "understood" a few hundred times in the past, let's assume I understand this time. The issue of firearms. It's a big step. It has to be supervised. The chief constable says you have to supervise it. I'm with you that far. I can understand it up to that point. But twenty-four hours a day? Till further notice? You must be out of your mind.'

'We don't know when it'll come,' said Sullivan hoarsely.

'There's a telephone here. An extension alongside the bed. If anything happens, if you're needed, they can always . . .'

'The time it takes to get from here to headquarters. It could make all the difference.'

'Between what?' scoffed Steve. 'Hitting or missing?'

'Cut it out, Steve.' Sullivan's voice was tired, as if he was indeed too old to do battle. He said, 'I know you mean well. I know you're arguing on behalf of your mother. But . . .' He shrugged, turned to his wife, and said, 'Mary, this is a big can. Too big for anybody else to carry. He's killed twice, one of 'em a senior police officer, so we need guns to make sure he doesn't kill again. But we don't *like* guns. Innocent people might get hurt. Might even get killed. That's why. Somebody has to be there on the spot to make the decisions. I've been given the job.'

'And we don't count?' said his wife, wearily.

'Count? Of course you count. Both of you. But it has to be done this way, because any other way would be sloppy. I'll take over one of the rest rooms. The beds are comfortable enough. The canteen serves good grub. It'll only be for a few days. Until we're absolutely sure. I'll phone every day to let you know . . .'

'Don't bother.' Mary Sullivan's voice was flat with defeat. 'This telephone doesn't get answered till you come home. And when you *do* come home, when you've finished this silly game of cowboys and indians, don't be too surprised. Don't be too surprised if nobody's here waiting for you.'

The killer spent Sunday night at Preston. On the Monday he caught a bus north to Lancaster, and from there another bus to Morecambe. He spent the Monday night at Morecambe.

He was travelling. Running, he supposed. But running from what? From the police? No, he was pretty sure the police hadn't enough to go on to prove any real hazard. The gun? Nothing less than a miracle could trace him via the gun, he'd been far too careful for that. The sight and the mounting? No, never in a hundred years. He'd bought one in Birmingham and the other in Nottingham. He'd used two false names, he'd paid cash, he'd grown a beard, bought the sight, then shaved off the beard and worn specs when he'd bought the mount. Simple, basic precautions. But the gun and the sight and the mount wouldn't lead the police to him, to *anybody*. The mac? That could lead to a thousand men. Ten thousand. It was identical with twenty-five per cent of the macs bought and sold in the U.K. And he'd never been finger-printed. Not once.

There was nothing. Not one damn thing.

And yet, he was running.

Fear was part of it. Unnecessary fear, but necessary or not, a very real fear. A fear bordering upon panic. That he *might* not be as safe as he thought he was. That there *might* be some tiny thing he'd overlooked.

And Kim? Supposing *she* guessed. What would *she* do?

Not that there was anything to make Kim suspicious. Her no more than the police. She didn't know about the gun and the mac, so if they published a photograph of it, which indeed they might do, it wouldn't mean a thing.

154

It was a mac. An ordinary, common-or-garden mac. Kim might see it. So what? To her it would be just that; a photograph of a mac . . . not *his* mac.

And yet, despite all his self-persuasion, Kim was still part of his fear. And fear kept him running.

Fear and guilt.

Oh yes, guilt came into the scheme of things too. Very much into the scheme of things. Two killings. You can't kill twice and not feel guilt. He'd thought it possible. Indeed, he'd counted on the certainty that what the world had done to him would have made him impervious to such feelings. Being kicked in the teeth. Being ground under. Being smashed and dishonoured and for no good reason. Why the hell should such a man feel guilt? Why? Because he was a complete man. Because he was an animal – a biped – but not a beast.

Fear and guilt, and a certain inability to concentrate.

Preston. What was Preston? And *why* Preston? Because the train had been going to Preston. The first train to leave Lessford, the first transport available to rush him away from the iniquity, had been a train whose destination had been Preston. That was the reason. The only reason. He didn't know Preston. He'd never before halted at the place. Previously he'd known it only as the bottle-neck cursed by drivers making their way to the west coast holiday resorts: Preston, the utterly inadequate 'ring road' and the series of bridges and countless traffic lights. That had been Preston.

That still *was* Preston.

He'd spent the night at a small side-street hotel. Hotel? Ah well, the name 'hotel' covered many things. This one had been a staging post for down-at-heel reps. A place of poor meals, hard beds in tiny bedrooms and a breakfast surrounded by middle-aged men, all wearing that same expression of near-terrified frustration.

155

Then from Preston to Lancaster, and from Lancaster to Morecambe.

Monday, the old Bank Holiday Monday, in Morecambe. An odd place. Not as gaudy, not as brash, not as openly expensive – or as expansive – as its neighbour, Blackpool. Not as many drunks, not as many cheapjack stalls, not as many shows. Not as many anything. Crowds. But not the surging, candy-floss-carrying, rock-munching, laughing, singing crowds of Blackpool. The sea was there, of course. The same dirty-grey sea. The Irish Channel and Morecambe Bay, with Barrow away in the distance, like a darker greyness rising from the grey of the sea.

And beyond the greyness, beyond the Irish Channel, beyond Ireland herself : the Atlantic. And somewhere beyond the Atlantic a place called Moose Jaw.

He'd stood at the shoreline, the wavelets rippling up to his feet like a million tiny, silent bells, and he'd watched. Seen in his mind's eye. Beyond the horizon. Beyond the clouds, even. A town – a haven – with a strange and fascinating name. A town he didn't know and couldn't describe. His own particular Oz, but without the yellow-brick road along which he might travel to get there.

At dusk he'd wandered away from the sea. Found a dingy boarding-house with the sign 'Vacancies' propped up in the window.

And there he'd spent Monday night. Alone in a bed which gave little comfort. In 'a room whose window looked out on to a row of yards, each with its quota of over-filled dustbins. A miserable place which reflected his own misery.

Preston, Lancaster and Morecambe. Running. Running from nothing and running to nowhere.

*

They buried Wrie on the Monday.

The grave was in a churchyard out in the Yorkshire countryside, at a village where he'd been born and where his parents, too, had been born. The vicar had baptized him and was now burying him.

'Man that is born of a woman hath but a short time to live, and is full of misery.'

The undertaker's men stooped, picked up the ends of the canvas strips, and eased the coffin clear of the battens.

'He cometh up, and is cut down like a flower; he fleeth as it were a shadow, and never continueth in one stay.'

'The grave-diggers moved in, unobtrusively, and pulled the battens from their place across the grave. The undertaker's men allowed the canvas strips to run through their fingers and the coffin slowly, and a little wobbly, began its descent into the hole.

The mourners watched, or did not watch, as the fancy took them. Those who watched concentrated their attention on the silver plate upon which was etched the name, the date of birth and the date of death. Those who did not watch pretended to watch; they stood with bowed heads, aimed their eyes at the lowering coffin, but kept their gaze deliberately out of focus.

'In the midst of life we are in death; of whom may we seek for succour, but thee, O Lord, who for our sins art justly displeased?'

The mourners stood on clay-stained boards surrounding the grave, and the boards were positioned around the grave on the mounds of soil and clay which had been dug from the grave.

The women wore black, complete with black hats, and a few of the hats had veils. The men wore dark suits, navy blue serge or dark grey, with black ties against the white shirts. Some held their hats in their hands; dark-coloured felt hats and, in one case, a bowler. Clothes

bought for the occasion or, if not, for previous inter-
ments; necropolic uniforms, as necessary and as formal
as the winding-sheet.

'*Yet, O Lord God most holy, O Lord most mighty, O
holy and most merciful Saviour, deliver us not into the
bitter pains of eternal death.*'

The words were uttered without real feeling. An incan-
tation without power, without solace, without enchant-
ment. A recital of vowels and consonants, repeated for
the umpteenth time and in a voice, away from the
resonant surrounds of the church, which sounded weedy
and mildly ridiculous.

A handkerchief fluttered here and there. A tiny square
of lace-fringed linen, white against the black of the
mourning regalia.

The undertaker bent to pick a handful of loose soil
from the edge of the surrounding mounds and eased
himself into the knot of mourners ringing the grave. His
men released the canvas strips as the coffin rested upon
the ochre-coloured floor of the grave.

'*Thou knowest, Lord, the secrets of our hearts; shut
not thy merciful ears to our prayer; but spare us, Lord
most holy, O God most mighty.*'

A man blew his nose. Noisily and on a huge, blue
handkerchief. A woman sniffled as she wept; weeping
because it was seemly to weep on such occasions and because she wept easily.

Richard Wrie and Mabel Wrie stood, side by side, on
the boards above the head of the coffin. Pale-faced. Dry-
eyed. Holding hands in the tiny, private world of misery
only they inhabited.

'*O holy and merciful Saviour, thou most worthy Judge
eternal, suffer us not, at our last hour, for any pains of
death, to fall from thee.*'

The undertaker leaned forward and tossed the handful
of earth into the grave. It landed with a tiny clatter on

the lid of the coffin. A child, not knowing what she was doing or why, was nudged forward by her mother and dropped a tiny posy of flowers on to the scattered earth which now marked the polished surface of the coffin.

'*Forasmuch as it hath pleased Almighty God of his great mercy to take unto himself the soul of our dear brother here departed, we therefore commit his body to the ground; earth to earth, ashes to ashes, dust to dust; in sure and certain hope of the Resurrection to eternal life, through our Lord Jesus Christ; who shall change our vile body, that it may be like unto his glorious body, according to the mighty working, whereby he is able to subdue all things to himself.*'

Thus it went, and thus it continued and was, eventually, concluded. The words from The Book of Common Prayer. 'The Order for the Burial of the Dead.' Unchanged since the death of Edward VI; the ritualistic offer of official comfort, which so rarely gave any comfort at all.

The girl standing by the lychgate, alone and out of earshot, watched and waited.

The mourners wandered away from the graveside. They walked in pairs and in tiny groups. There was a last shuffle along the planking surrounding the hole, an almost timid gesture of last respect, then with some relief, or so it seemed, a slow stroll up the path between the gravestones and towards the gate. The men's hats were returned to their heads, and the women's handkerchiefs returned to their handbags. Two of the men lit cigarettes, open evidence of their relief of the ending of a required duty.

The mother walked, bowed-headed, between her husband and the vicar.

The girl stepped forward and said, 'Mrs. Wrie . . . ,' then stopped, because she had no notion of how to say all the things she wanted to say.

The trio halted and the mother raised her head and looked into the face of her dead son's mistress.

'You,' she said, softly. 'You've the impudence to come here. Here. Today.'

The vicar said, 'Mrs. Wrie, I'm sure . . .'

'If it wasn't for *you* . . .' The mother's voice gained in strength. Life returned to her eyes, a life filled with hatred and heartbreak. She ignored the vicar, ignored the look of concern on her husband's face and said, 'He'd have been with us. Holidaying. He's never missed. Not once, since he was a bairn. But you made him. You offered him dirt and he was too weak to refuse. That's why he's . . .' She jerked her head. 'That's why he's *there*.'

Then the mother spat. A tiny spray of spittle which reached the girl's face and made her jerk her head backwards.

Richard Wrie said, 'Nay, lass! For God's sake. There's no call for . . .'

His wife didn't hear him. She was already five paces away and being caught up with by the vicar. The odd thing was that none of the other mourners seemed to have noticed the incident.

Wrie took a newly laundered handkerchief from his pocket, held it out to the girl and said, 'Look, lass . . . I'm sorry. She – she didn't mean it. She's not herself. Can you blame her? She didn't mean it, though.'

The girl shook out the handkerchief and used it to wipe the tiny marks of spittle from her face.

She said, 'Thanks, Mr. Wrie. But she meant it. And I don't blame her.'

'Guns,' said the beefy detective sergeant.

'You sell 'em,' added the equally beefy detective constable.

The two men seemed to fill the small and cluttered gunsmith's shop. Like frogs expanding their throats in a courtship routine, the duo of detectives seemed to swell until the floorspace had the appearance of wall-to-wall coppers.

The gunsmith agreed that he sold guns.

This was policing the Birmingham way; 'Brum' being a city whose law-enforcement called for a certain no-messing-about panache. The villains of this city had a reputation. They chewed nails and spat rust, or so they thought. They came in all colours and all sizes, but to a man they were hard cases, or so they thought. They caused the wooden-tops to shake in their size tens and ensured that the dicks wet their nappies at the very mention of their names, or so they thought.

Or so they thought.

The C.I.D. of Birmingham thought otherwise and, with almost boring regularity, the C.I.D. of Birmingham proved that they were right. Thanks to men like the D.S. and the D.C.

'Why the sweat?' asked the D.S.

The gunsmith denied that he was sweating.

'You been up to something?' asked the D.C.

'You don't seem too pleased to see us,' observed the D.S.

'As if we weren't welcome,' added the D.C.

The gunsmith stuttered and stammered the usual string of false denials; that he had nothing to hide; that he *liked* the police; that there was nothing – *nothing* – he wasn't prepared to tell the police or show the police.

The detectives knew their man. Guns were bought and guns were sold, all manner of guns up to, and including, second war Stens. And ammunition for these guns. The bang-bang boys obtained their toys from somewhere, and where else but from a gunsmith? *This* gunsmith. They lacked the proof. They had the knowledge, too many narks had opened their snivelling little cake-holes, but funny-man here had so far out-smarted them. Neverthe-less, they *knew*.

The D.S. unfolded a piece of paper, placed it on the counter and said, 'This.'

The gunsmith read the few words and numbers on the piece of paper and looked up wonderingly.

'You sold it,' said the D.S.

'Please,' added the D.C. in a bored voice, 'don't spin the fanny. *You* sold it. The manufacturers keep records. It was delivered to this shop. It's not in this shop now. You sold it.'

'Or gave it away. Or swapped it,' murmured the D.S.

The gunsmith moistened his lips, then admitted that he had, at various times, sold Leupold M7-4x telescopic sights. That was his business, wasn't it? That was what the shop was for, to sell guns and accessories.

'When?' asked the D.S.

The gunsmith couldn't remember.

'Who to?' asked the D.C.

The gunsmith couldn't remember.

'You're playing silly buggers,' warned the D.S.

The gunsmith assured the D.S. that he *never* played silly buggers.

'The law requires you to keep records,' said the D.C.

Ah, yes, records. But of *firearms*, not of telescopic sights. Some people bought telescopic sights for other reasons. To fit on long-range cameras, for example.

The D.S. said, 'Bollocks.'

The D.C. said, 'Knackers.'

The D.S. said, 'V.A.T. returns.'

The gunsmith agreed that he submitted V.A.T. re-turns, or to be accurate, his accountant submitted them on his behalf. All he did was make out the cheque. But, unfortunately, V.A.T. returns didn't record names and addresses of customers, much less their descriptions. He was sorry. He was very sorry, but he couldn't remember. Anything!

The D.S. sucked his teeth meditatively for a moment, then said, 'One day you'll remember, chummy. By Christ, will *you* remember! It'll all come back, in a flood. It'll choke you. And I'll be there, right there alongside you, to make damn sure nobody gives you artificial respiration.'

The gunsmith at Nottingham was chalk to the Birmingham man's cheese. He was one of the most respected men in the town and recognised as such by the police.

A uniformed sergeant visited him.

Records were consulted and the gunsmith said, 'Yes, it's here. About a year ago. A Detacho-Mount locking device. Same number. Paid for in cash. I have the receipt number if that'll help.'

'A description,' said the sergeant. 'That's what *I* want. As good a description of the man who bought it as possible. His name and address, if you've got it.'

'Smith.' The gunsmith consulted his records. 'Thomas Smith.'

'Oh, my God, Alf!' protested the sergeant.

'Some people *are* called Smith,' said the gunsmith, gently. 'Even Thomas Smith.'

'And the address? Don't tell me Buck House.'

'No address.' The gunsmith grinned. 'Just the name for the receipt.'

'Remember him?'

'I dunno.' The gunsmith frowned his concentration. 'I sell a fair number of Detacho-Mounts. They're good. They're popular. I average about one a fortnight.'

'It's important,' urged the sergeant.

'Well, he paid cash.' The gunsmith moved his finger along the written record of sale. 'Beyond that, nothing.

I'm sorry. Nothing outstanding, otherwise I'd have remembered.'

'No address?'

'Sorry. Cash.'

'Bloody hell.'

On the Tuesday, they cremated Rucker.

Gilliant and Bear were there. So were Lennox and Sugden. The press and the TV newsreel boys covered the ceremony and, as the tiny party walked from the crematorium chapel, one of the television interviewers ignored good taste and held a microphone towards the mouth of Mrs. Rucker.

The TV man said, 'Can I ask you for your immediate reaction to the murder of your husband, Mrs. Rucker?'

'You can ask.' She stopped, brushed aside Gilliant and Sugden who made as if to shift the impeding media man. She said, 'You can ask. But what do you expect as an answer?'

'You want the murderer caught. Obviously.'

'Obviously.'

'On a personal basis, I mean?' The TV man grew fractionally bolder.

'On a personal basis,' she replied, flatly.

'And – er – your opinion on capital punishment, Mrs. Rucker?'

'It doesn't count for anything.'

'Surely.' He smiled, knowingly. 'The return of hanging for the murder of policemen? That's what I mean.'

She looked squarely into the lens of the watching camera and, in a very steady voice, said, 'The question's impertinent, but I'll answer it. In any situation. *Any* situation. If somebody *has* to be killed, if there's no other way, I think it should be a policeman. He's paid to protect the public. With his life, if necessary. My husband knew that. Every policeman knows it. If he doesn't he should.'

'Which means?' teased the TV man.

'No.' She gave him a smile, tinged with permafrost. 'Put your own interpretation on it.'

He became even more bold.

He said, 'There aren't many mourners, Mrs. Rucker.'

The answer was a classic and later that evening it was beamed out over the whole U.K.

She said, 'If that's an observation, it's superfluous. If it's a criticism, I suggest you wait until you can have a head-count at *your* funeral.'

Sullivan slept in one of the trio of so-called 'rest rooms' at the Lessford M.P.D. Headquarters. So-called because strictly speaking they had never been intended as places for prolonged stays. They each had a more-or-less comfortable single bed, they had corner washbasins with a plentiful supply of hot water, they had bedside cabinets, tiny wardrobes, mirrors and plugs for electric razors. But even so they were never meant to be *lived* in. Their purpose was that of a stop-gap; a place where over-tired officers might cat-nap and freshen themselves up should a case come to a temporary halt, but with not enough time available to get home for a proper rest.

Previously such officers had camped on one of the beds in an empty cell. These 'rest rooms' were an improvement, but that's all they were meant to be.

Sullivan, however, moved in and, as the days passed, he became aware of a very embarrassing spin-off. He was becoming unpopular. He was getting in everybody's way.

As one work-weary detective sergeant muttered, 'Christ, he's never *away* from the bloody place. It's bad enough without having a deputy chief treading on your tail twenty-four hours a day.'

Thus, Sullivan. A man once popular, a man once almost beloved of the men over whom he wielded authority and now becoming more unpopular by the day. One might almost say, by the hour.

Sullivan was learning things.

That the tactician is often a poor strategist; that the sergeant who can lead his platoon into a nest of enemy firepower is, perhaps, the last man capable of carrying a field-marshal's baton. And, in the present situation, the man that was once supreme as a chief superintendent in charge of the toughest division in Lessford was not now capable of delegating responsibility with the assurance of a deputy chief constable.

On the Tuesday evening Bear sat on the bed while Sullivan stretched out in the armchair he'd borrowed from the canteen and they talked. Their talk was at first of the case. Then it expanded to include opinions and theories of policing in general.

At last it turned to specifics.

Bear said, 'Take a breather. I'll stay here for the night.'

'No.'

Sullivan's one-word answer was dogmatic. Not because he didn't welcome the opportunity of a break, but because to do so would have somehow lowered himself in his own esteem. Childish? A grown man, indeed a man reaching the last of the middle-years, indulging in the crackbrained pastime of 'showing his muscles'? Possibly. But there in the background was Mary Sullivan. And Steve. In effect, if not in as many words, they'd both hinted that he was over the hill. That his days of *real* bobbying were finished. Gone. Just like that. That he was now a figurehead. A rubber-stamp. A man no longer capable of holding his corner.

Bear said, 'It'll please Mary.'

'I don't doubt that.'

'In that case . . .'

'I'm not paid to "please Mary".' Sullivan's tone was gruff. Almost unfriendly. He said, 'The chief constable ordered firearms. A picked squad. He put me in charge.'

'For Christ's sake, I can . . .'

'I'm not saying you can't. Just that he detailed me.'

'It could go on,' argued Bear.

'It could.'

'For weeks. For months.'

'I doubt it. No more than a fortnight. Three weeks at the most. Then there'll be a stand-down.'

'Three weeks!' Bear stared. 'You mean you're prepared to hole up here for three weeks?'

'If necessary. Longer if necessary.'

Bear rubbed the nape of his neck, frowned, then chose his words with care.

He said, 'Dick, you're not helping matters.'

'I'm obeying orders.'

'No. I don't mean that.' Bear waved a hand awkwardly. 'Not that. Gilliant wants you here. Okay, that's an order. But the men . . .'

Bear ran out of words.

'What about the men?'

'Those in the Operations Centre. They're on edge.'

'What the hell . . . ?'

'Look, you know what it's like.' Bear tried hard to explain. 'At the divisional dances. The social nights. We put in an appearance. Gilliant. You. Me. Sugden. Harris. But only an *appearance*. We don't stay. We arrive, we say "Hello", then we leave. We don't want to screw up the festivities.'

Sullivan growled, 'What the hell's that to do with a murder enquiry? Are you suggesting they have a social night in the Operations Centre when they aren't supervised?'

'For God's sake.'

'That's what you're saying.'

'You're cramping their style, Dick.' Bear decided to be blunt. To be hurtful if necessary. He said, 'They get things done. The working coppers. They cut corners sometimes. Forget the book. But they get things done. They keep the enquiry moving.'

'That's all I'm asking.'

'You're slamming the brake on. Hard,' said Bear. 'You're around. Here, inside this building. Twenty-four hours. Night and day. Nobody's going to chance his arm, not with a deputy chief constable breathing down his neck.'

'Meaning they don't trust me?' Genuine shock showed on Sullivan's face.

'Meaning they *daren't* trust you.' Bear sounded almost desperate. 'God Almighty, Dick. Remember when you were an ordinary copper. Or a sergeant. Or even an inspector. You did things – we all did things – scores of times. Things we wouldn't have even thought of doing with the big boys within sniffing distance.'

'Not with guns.' Sullivan deliberately misunderstood.

Bear tried, but Bear was fighting something well beyond his own appreciation. Sullivan was a good man, a fine copper, but in the wrong job. And the job itself carried overtones of age. It conjured up pictures of flash offices and comfortable chairs and a leader, leading from a safe distance in the rear.

It was what Mary Sullivan had hinted at. And Steve. And now Bear.

Therefore, Bear tried, but Bear failed.

And the days and nights of the week crawled their way into contemporary history. The killings left the front page and, by Wednesday, they were merely mentioned within the junk which went to make the centre pages of the dailies. Even *The Lessford and Bordfield Tribune* turned its attention to other things and, in a double column on page two, merely re-hashed what was already known about the Wrie – Rucker murders.

Hot news became old news.

The force reorganized itself a little. Sugden and Harris worked out a rough-and-ready shift system; men and women were allowed to catch up on sleep; most of the temporary plainclothes officers were returned to uniform, to re-establish themselves as recognized sign-posts of law; the net widened via messages to other forces in the U.K. along the Express Message system but, with the widening of the net, the mesh became larger.

Every lead was followed : every whispered hint and crank telephone message was attended to and every lead led into one more blind alley.

A subtle lethargy set in.

In the Operations-Centre-cum-Recreation-Room the paper still collected. The filing cabinets filled and the cross-references were kept up to date. But that first, heady, breakneck urgency filtered away. Now it was a matter of waiting. A matter of patience. A matter of sifting and re-examining the mass of data already collected. The break which would galvanise every man and woman into action. The hint, the clue, which might identify this mysterious 'John Doe'.

And for how long?

Well, it sometimes took months. Sometimes even years. The old hands knew this; that, as time passed, the Recreation Room would once more be a Recreation Room; that the mountain of paper would be shifted into some hole-in-the-corner office, somewhere (probably not even within the headquarters building), and that gradually the man-power would be lessened until eventually one solitary detective constable would be left, to stand guard upon all this useless bumph, bored to hell and merely checking and re-checking that the various statements and reports were in their correct slots inside the filing cabinets.

A murder file is never marked 'closed' until the culprit has been brought to justice.

Great! To that extent, it *isn't*. But the fiction must be guyed up to give the appearance of fact. And that's how it's done and that's how it was going to be done, unless something pretty big cracked in the very near future.

The sheer magnitude of the initial man-hunt insisted that this must happen. Coppers have other things to do; they can't spend every hour of every day racing around chasing murderers of whom they know damn-all. Without the periodic, and fairly regular, flick of genuine 'further information', the wheel *had* to slow down and the slowing down process couldn't be delayed too long; the back-log of other and lesser crimes was a brake which could not be ignored.

A murder enquiry, then. Two men slaughtered by the same gun; therefore, presumably, by the same killer. The initial spit and sparkle. But by the Thursday it had been reduced to a dull ache of frustration.

THURSDAY – AUGUST 4th

I would ask you. I would beg you to believe me. I am not an evil man; I care not what the newsrags say : I am *not* an evil man !

It was not I who placed cash before human life. It was not I who ignored a letter, couched in simple, easy-to-understand language. Ten thousand pounds. That's all I asked for – a mere ten thousand. Had it been paid, that might have been the end of the matter. No killings. No police cordon from which I must escape. The youth Wrie would not have died. Nor would the policeman Rucker. A paltry ten thousand pounds. But they forced me to kill, then they forced me to increase the amount, then they forced me to kill again. *They* did. The fools. The 'establishment' cretins to whom human life means nothing; to whom each man, woman and child is a mere statistic.

To keep their money, to ensure that the fiscal god remained on his throne, they sacrificed two lives.

It tells everything.

They or their kind sacrificed a fine firm on the same altar of greed. Compassion is missing from their makeup. Even good sense . . . they are blind to its simple logic. They sacrificed a firm, they sacrificed a good man, my son-in-law, in part they sacrificed his wife in that when they placed him behind prison walls she, too, died a little, they sacrificed a young, innocent man and a senior police officer. The same people. Various facets of the same madness. An officialdom which pays lip-service to the priceless truths of democracy but which, in fact, pays true homage to the inhumanity of the hammer and sickle.

As cold-blooded as the K.G.B. As ruthlessly determined as the Kremlin. Our government, our masters, our 'system', which in the final analysis drove me to perform an act of which I am, perhaps, ashamed.

Ashamed . . . and yet not ashamed. Mine was the gun which killed. Mine was the finger on the trigger. But the driving force? Ah, the driving force. That was not mine.

All I asked for was peace. To be left alone, to make my small mark on the world and, in the doing thereof, provide good men with a good living. I was no part of a grand plan; no vital cog in some vast and complex machine. My responsibility began and ended within the limits of a tiny, provincial engineering firm; a firm which produced fine and accurate products, turned and fashioned by skilled men.

That's what I was. That's all I ever wanted to be. But they – 'them' – refused me even *that*.

And now I am without anchor, without base, without stability.

From Lessford to Preston. From Preston to Lancaster. From Lancaster to Morecambe. From Morecambe to Manchester. And now from Manchester to Bordfield. So near home. So near my starting point. A circle, an irregular circle which has brought me back to Point 'A'. A thing without anchor and without stability, that is what I have become.

But also without guilt.

The guilt is not mine. The guilt belongs to a very impersonal thing called 'the system'. Tangle with 'the system', my friend, and that is the end. You're finished. You cease to exist. You are *gone*, blown off the face of this good earth like a dust mote.

Like me.

The money I salvaged from the bankrupt firm, plus

the money obtained by the sale of Mabel's shares, before the official receiver knocked on the door is running out. I started with sufficient; not enough to take me to Moose Jaw, but sufficient. I have nursed it. Walked, when I might have taken a bus. Slept in dingy houses and on dirty beds. Eaten as little as possible. Sought shelter in library reading rooms. Spent nothing – *nothing* – other than what was necessary, but already my pathetic bundle of bank notes is noticeably thinner.

And I am here. Almost at my starting point.

I must take stock of things. I must pause to think. A way, a way in which I might beat that infernal 'system'.

2.57 p.m.

Again, the timing was very accurate. The call was logged by the switchboard operator, then passed through to Tallboy in the Operations-Centre-cum-Recreation-Room.

Tallboy said, 'Inspector Tallboy, here.'

'John Doe.'

'Who?'

As he asked the unnecessary question Tallboy seemed to jerk into action. He snapped his fingers to attract the attention of Sullivan, who was standing two table-lengths away, then pointed to the mouthpiece of the telephone he was holding and silently, and with much exaggeration, mouthed the words 'It's *him*.'

Sullivan allowed himself a single nod of understanding, then literally pounced upon the second telephone which had been set up in the room.

'John Doe,' said the voice.

'Oh!'

'I still want that money.'

'That's – er – that's to be understood,' fenced Tallboy.

*

Shielding the mouthpiece with his hand, Sullivan used a low but urgent tone.

'This is the police. Deputy Chief Constable Sullivan. I want some fast action. There's a call coming through on the other phone in this Operations Centre. I want to know where it's being made from.'

'I'll put you through to the Telephone Area Office, sir.'

'For Christ's sake.'

'Fifty thousand pounds.'

'That was the sum agreed upon,' confirmed Tallboy.

'And this time I don't want to have to shoot a copper.'

'No. Nor do we.'

'Telephone Area Office. Can I help you?'

'The police here. Get me on to whoever's in charge.'

'If you'll give me some idea of what the complaint . . .'

'*Fast!*'

'Er – yes, sir. A Mr. Broadbent. I'll put you through.'

'You still have the money?'

'We can – er . . . We can get it. If necessary,' parried Tallboy.

'It's necessary.'

'Within reason, of course.'

'What the hell d'you mean? Within reason?'

'It's a lot of money.'

'You've got it.'

"No. We *had* it. When you shot Chief Superintendent Rucker.'

'Mr. Broadbent. Can I . . . ?'

'Deputy Chief Constable Sullivan, here. There's a

temporary phone. Er – Bordfield four-nine-three-nine-two. Set up by you people here, in headquarters. Somebody's on that line. I want to know where from before he rings off.'

'Hold the line, please. I'll see what I can do.'

'Look, if you're trying to blind me with bullshit, Longfellow, or what the hell your name is . . .'

'Tallboy. Detective Inspector Tallboy.'

'Okay. Tallboy. If you're . . .'

'But, I'm not. Of course I'm not.'

Tallboy frowned worried urgency across at Sullivan and Sullivan replied with tightened lips, widened nostrils and a look of utter disgust.

'Just remember. Eh?'

'That you've already killed twice?'

'I can make it three, very easily.'

'Quite. But, presumably, you'd prefer the money? The fifty thousand pounds?'

'Not prefer it. I'm gonna *get* it.'

'Of course. But first we'll have to get it.'

'I thought . . .'

'We haven't the facilities to hold that amount of cash here. It was returned to the bank.'

'Ah, Mr. Sullivan. Broadbent here, again.'

'Where the flaming hell . . . ?'

'You're fortunate. We have a man at the automatic exchange. I've been in touch. Cawdale Rise. There's a kiosk, near the main entrance to the iron foundry. About half-way along Fitzwilliam Street. That's where . . .'

'I know it. Thanks.'

Sullivan dropped the receiver, gave a quick thumbs-up sign to Tallboy and ran from the Operations-Centre-cum-Recreation-Room.

*

'You'd better get it out again, copper. You'd better get it out again, fast.'

'Or what?' Tallboy played it by ear, knowing that every second added to the telephonic exchange was gold-plated.

'You crazy?'

'I'm asking a straightforward question. What if we don't get the money as quickly as last time? What if we *can't*?'

'You're gonna have a stiff on your hands. *That's* what.'

'It might not be as easy as last time.'

'Why the hell ...?'

'The bank might not co-operate as readily.'

'If they know what's good for 'em ...'

'The bank? It doesn't affect them, one way or the other.'

Sullivan took the stairs to the top floor of headquarters building, two at a time. He burst into the Radio Operations Room and, almost before the door was fully open, he was bawling instructions to the sergeant in charge.

'Every car, within a five-mile radius of Cawdale Rise area. Converge on Fitzwilliam Street. Now! I want it blocked off. Side streets, everything. Patrol cars, C.I.D. cars, the lot. And as many foot patrol men as possible. Nothing in, nothing out, till further orders. But no medal-chasing. John Doe's in the telephone kiosk by the iron foundry. He's dangerous. He might be armed. Our own armed men are on the way.'

Before the sergeant had acknowledged the instructions with a 'Yes, sir,' a uniformed policewoman had flicked toggles and was already speaking into the microphone.

'All cars within a five-mile radius of Cawdale Rise. All cars. This is an urgent message. Number One Priority.'

*

Tallboy was replacing the receiver as Sullivan arrived back at the Operations-Centre-cum-Recreation-Room.

Tallboy began, 'I kept him on as long as possible, but . . .'

'Long enough,' interrupted Sullivan. He weaved his way past tables, towards a corner cupboard and, at the same time, fished keys from the pocket of his trousers. He said, 'The other two gun experts. Are they alerted?'

One of the clerks said, 'I've warned 'em, sir. They were in the billiards room. They should be waiting in the car.'

'Good.' Sullivan unlocked the cupboard, opened its doors and took out three holstered .45 magnum, six-shot, Smith & Wesson revolvers. He dumped the firearms on an adjacent table, then placed an unopened box of cartridges alongside them. He growled, 'Take your pick, inspector. We'll load on the way.'

3.10 p.m.

Sullivan drove. Alongside him, Tallboy thumbed rounds into the cylinder of the revolver; one round into each of five chambers, leaving an empty chamber as a long-stop safety factor, the empty chamber being the first chamber to take the firing-pin. They were fat, squat rounds; magnums, with that extra punch which hoisted a .45 slug well beyond the 'superficial wound' category. Man-stoppers, whichever part of the anatomy they hit.

Tallboy closed the cylinder, then passed the box of cartridges to the two uniformed officers in the rear. A uniformed sergeant and a uniformed constable; middle-aged, cool-headed men; prepared to shoot if necessary, but also prepared *not* to shoot until it *became* necessary.

Sullivan weaved a racing path along the centre of the carriageway. The revolving blue lamp, on the roof of the car, and the nerve-shaking bellow of the 'gong' demanding unrestricted right of passage.

Real cops-and-robbers stuff. Real T.V. dramatics, except that Sullivan hated the idea of British bobbies being armed.

Guns were everywhere, these days. They were damn near a give-away gimmick with packets of crisps. Too many bloody guns : revolvers, pistols, sawn-off shotguns; a damn sight too many guns. Wild West stuff; the brand of argument which had spawned that black humoured remark, 'God made men, but Sam Colt made them equal.' Weeping Judas! They were back at Square One again; the quick-on-the-trigger lunacy where the biggest bastards had to be bought and given badges in order to tame the lesser bastards. And the Yanks had never grown out of it. That was why their coppers carried guns, why the transatlantic villains had *always* carried guns. A legacy from the O.K. Corral, something like that.

And now it had arrived here. The 'shooters' went with just about every cock-up the various comedians contrived. And consequently even the good old British 'wooden-tops' had, when the occasion demanded it, to cart guns around with them.

The trouble was, as Sullivan saw it, guns bred more guns. The lawless used guns, therefore the law-enforcers were obliged to use guns. The law-enforcers used guns, therefore even more of the lawless figured that guns were part of the general game. It was a spiral and there was a point of no-return, and that point had been passed years back. Guns now *were* part of the game and Sullivan hated the idea.

As he handled the wheel, and wound the squad car through the traffic, he said, 'No shooting, unless necessary. And no killing. Aim for the legs. Below the knee, if possible.'

The loudspeaker changed its background tone of static, then a voice said, 'D.C.C. Sullivan. How do you hear me, please?'

Tallboy unclipped the mike and said, 'Loud and clear. Go ahead, please.'

The voice said, 'Message from patrol cars at scene. Probable suspect spotted. Believed to have been seen leaving the kiosk. He ran for it. Officer sending report gives it as his opinion that the suspect is armed.'

Sullivan breathed, 'Christ!'

Tallboy asked, 'Which direction was suspect heading for, when last seen?'

The voice from the loudspeaker answered, 'Into the foundry, we think.'

'Okay.' Tallboy didn't wait for Sullivan's instructions. He said, 'Tell all units to converge on the foundry. Cordon it off, but remain outside till we arrive. Notify the foundry management of the situation and tell them to warn their employees to keep under cover till further notice.'

The voice said, 'Will do', and the background static from the speaker switched back to its previous tone.

'And if he ain't in the foundry?' asked Sullivan, brusquely.

'I get a rocket up my arse . . . sir.'

3.22 p.m.

He was in the foundry.

The squad car parked at the main entrance verified that fact. The indignant driver pointed to a shattered headlamp and a flattened front tyre as proof that, (a) he was in the foundry, and (b) he was armed.

'The gun-happy bastard,' complained the driver then, remembering the rank, continued, 'Beg pardon, sir. But, dammit, we were pulling to a halt, then he let fly.'

'Where was he?' asked Sullivan.

'Up there, sir.' The squad car man nodded in the general direction of the sprawling mass and maze of heavy industrial plant which sprawled for acres across what at first gave the impression of an angular moonscape gone mad.

'*Up* there?' queried Tallboy.

'On one of the gantries, I think. He dodged out of sight as soon as he'd made his pot-shot.'

'Fine. Let's keep him up there. Away from ground level.'

Tallboy unholstered his revolver. The sergeant and the constable did likewise.

Sullivan said, 'The foundry workers?'

'They're all under cover, sir.' The squad car driver seemed to sigh, without actually sighing. 'They're *inside*. That's the most the management could do, sir. It's a semi-automatic plant, sir. It 'ud take all day to run down and almost a week to start up again. It's the best they could do.'

Sullivan grunted part-satisfaction, then asked, 'And our boys?'

'We have it covered on all sides, sir, pretty well.'

'Pretty well?'

'Er – almost, sir. Four more squad cars are on the way. Then it'll be ringed.'

The superintendent in charge of Cawdale Rise Division arrived in his Rover. He drew up alongside the parked squad car, gave Sullivan a perfunctory salute, then said, 'I just heard. I got here as soon as poss . . .'

'Keep this place sealed off, superintendent,' interrupted Sullivan. 'That's your job. This John Doe character. He's armed. We want him alive if possible, but we don't want any more coppers killed.' He glanced, sourly, at the already gathering groups of sightseers and added, 'And keep the bloody crowds back. Well back. Use the other divisions if necessary, but bring in as many men as you want. Nobody inside this plant. Nobody! We've three guns to his one. If we balls it up this time . . .'

3.25 p.m.

Sullivan wondered how the hell – *who* the hell – planned a place like this. A kid's construction set blown up to Gargantuan size, then having tons of fine, grey dust tipped over the whole damn set-up. Massive sheds and tall, flat, cone-shaped chimneys. Bloody great pipes, house-top high and apparently lagged to withstand a Siberian winter, winding and twisting overhead, linking one part of this bewildering conglomerate to another. Gantries and cat-walks everywhere, at a dozen different heights. And the stench of heat and sulphur and honest-to-God industry. Iron. Steel. This was where it was born. This was the frightening womb from which it was ejected. My God, small wonder it was one of the toughest of man-made materials ever produced.

And railway lines. Everywhere. Running into each other, branching off again, winding and snaking into, out of and alongside every smacking great hunk of this monument to 'heavy industry'. And all the bloody sleepers half-hidden in the layers of everlasting grey dust. You had to be careful, you could trip and come a real purler, if you didn't watch your feet.

Sullivan hated the place. The sheer size and complexity of the place both baffled and intimidated him. So many corners. So many potential hiding places. And somewhere among this lot . . .

The four men had split up. Tallboy had made a bent-backed dash for the shelter of a tumbledown brick shed, alongside the mass of railway lines. The sergeant and the constable had dodged away to the left; towards the side – perhaps the rear, if such a monstrosity had a 'rear' – in order to cover other possible escape routes.

The three 'guns' were tucked away and out of sight.

Sullivan, not deliberately nor from any conscious sense of heroism, offered himself as an unarmed target.

He walked carefully between railway lines and stacks of sheet metal. He squinted up at the dirty grey structures surrounding him, at the roofs and the cat-walks.

He stopped, cupped his hands to his mouth and yelled, 'Doe! John Doe! We know you're there. Come on out. Make it easy for yourself.'

Nobody answered.

Sullivan wished he'd brought a loud-hailer, contemplated a return to the main gate, in order to organize one, then changed his mind. He squinted up at the high-walled structures, at the lagged and dust-encrusted pipes, at the whole massive, complicated wherewithal via which ore was turned into metal.

3.35 p.m.

It was a waiting game. That much, already, was obvious. The quarry was somewhere within this modern ante-room to hell; somewhere, crouched and hidden, in any one of a thousand, ten thousand hole-outs. Sullivan paced the dusty and litter-strewn roadways, between the various 'sheds' of the plant. Nervous. On edge. But not consciously afraid.

The acrid smell of the place touched his nostrils and the back of his throat. God, to have to actually *work* here. To breathe this stuff in, eight hours a day, five days a week; year in, year out. Some men had lousy jobs and by comparison bobbying wasn't one of 'em. And this was only the *outside*. Christ only knew what it was like in there, where the actual smelting took place.

Periodically he paused in his prowling. Staring up at the mysterious structures towering above and watching for some sign of movement.

Every so often he cupped his hands to his mouth, and yelled, 'Doe! John Doe! Don't be a bloody fool. We know you're in there somewhere. Come on out. Get it over with.'

Stupid? Too true. This bastard had already killed twice and one of 'em a copper. This one wasn't going to be 'talked' out. He'd need to be flushed. And before nightfall, too. It was bad enough in daylight. Come night and, with all the floodlights in the world, the odds were in favour of Doe; the shadows would be even darker, the hiding places even more difficult to find. This one was going to have to be flushed – and with a damn sight more guns.

Sullivan reached a decision.

He turned to hurry back to the main entrance, there to organize more armed men for the hunt. And then he saw him. In full view. Racing along a high, iron cat-walk, for some new cover.

Sullivan yelled, 'Hey! Stop!' then he, too, ran. Parallel with the cat-walk, and parallel with the railway lines which ran beneath the cat-walk.

The man heard the shout, turned his head, paused,

made as if to raise the pistol he carried in his right hand, then changed his mind and raced ahead.

Sullivan bawled, 'Chris! Chris! He's up there. Above me.'

And all the time Sullivan pumped his legs into the near-ankle-deep dust in an attempt to keep level with the man on the cat-walk. Drawing in great lungfuls of the muck that was meant for air in this infernal place. Forcing himself forward. Glancing up to check that the quarry was still within sight, then switching his gaze to the ground in order not to stumble and sprawl across the debris of iron and clinker which scattered the ground. He could feel his chest tightening, as he forced himself to keep pace with this bastard John Doe; this killer of innocent young men called 'Steve'; this cop-killer who thought he could get away with it. He had to be kept in sight. He had to be caught. He had to be tamed. Damn and blast it, he had to be caught.

The man on the cat-walk seemed to sense the blind determination of his pursuer. He skidded to a halt, grabbed the single steel rail of the cat-walk, steadied himself, raised the pistol and fired.

Sullivan saw the movement. He tried to swerve. To force himself forward at an even faster speed, in order to spoil the aim.

Then he felt the pain. It hit his chest with all the force of a pile-driver and made him try to drag more air into his already bursting lungs. Then came the pain, an agony he had never thought possible. He tried to shout, but the simple weight of pain gagged him. He stubbed the toe of a shoe against a pile of clinker, but darkness had swamped him even before his face hit the thick dust of the yard.

3.40 p.m.

The uniformed sergeant had heard Sullivan's shouts. He was out from his hiding place, behind a parked railway wagon, before the man had stopped to fire a shot at Sullivan.

He squeezed the trigger of the Smith & Wesson once, to put a round in line with the firing pin and, as the man fired and Sullivan fell, the sergeant raised the .45 in a two-fisted grip and bawled, 'Hold it, there!'

The man on the cat-walk turned to meet his new enemy and, once more, squeezed the trigger of the pistol.

Things happened. Terrible things. The sergeant heard the slug from the pistol smack into the boards of the railway wagon. He held himself steady, knees slightly bent, and deliberately aimed for the man's legs. Below the knees. Two smooth squeezes on the trigger, as per range instruction. It was good aiming, damn good aiming. The sergeant saw one of the man's legs kicked backwards from under him as the bullet from the .45 found its mark. Saw the man drop the pistol, then stoop and try to retrieve it and, in doing so, lose his hold on the single rail of the cat-walk.

The sergeant saw the slope-sided, steel trucks move along the railway line beneath the cat-walk, and screamed, 'Hold on, man! Hold on!'

But the man couldn't. As his hand closed over the fallen pistol, the other hand grabbed for the rail and missed, and he toppled, head first, into the moving wagon.

The sergeant started an impossible dash towards the railway lines, realised its impossibility and stopped after about a dozen strides.

The truck moved forward into position. It stopped. The tall, square-sided maw opened and slowly, like an elongated rectangular tongue of shimmering white, over-woven with tie-dyed patterns of black, the molten waste and dross and clinker oozed out, crumbled, then fell in a fury of sparks into the waiting railway truck.

The maw closed. The air above the truck shimmered in the rising heat. Then the truck moved on to make way for its following companion.

SATURDAY – AUGUST 6th

4.30 p.m.

'If you think,' said Sullivan, 'I'm going to sit around on my fat arse, waiting for this thing to happen again, you've another think coming.'

Mary Sullivan smiled knowingly. There was a basis of worry in the smile, of course there was, but there was also a hint of contentment and, perhaps, the very ghost of something not too far removed from happiness.

Steve Sullivan, on the other hand, merely grinned.

'A bloody heart attack.' Sullivan's voice was weak and a trifle breathless. 'At a time like that. It scared the living daylights outa me. I thought the bastard had hit me.'

'A very *bad* heart attack,' Mary Sullivan reminded him gently.

'Like an old man,' muttered Sullivan, in disgust..

Steve's grin widened, and he said, 'You are an old man . . . old man.'

Sullivan tried to glare, but couldn't quite make it. Silently, he gave thanks for this son of his; for this member of a generation which refused to over-dramatise everything.

Nevertheless, there was a silent knowledge shared by the family Sullivan in that tiny side-ward. A knowledge which was never mentioned, but a knowledge which was absolute.

The days of bobbying were over.

Sullivan's face had the grey sheen of good putty. His eyes were a mite on the wild side, owing to the intake of drugs, and they seemed to rest wearily within the cavernous depths of darkened sockets. His hair was noticeably whiter than it had been a week before. Whiter and lifeless, as if his hair had died when that thrombosis had smacked home in his chest. It was uncombed and sprayed, untidily across the surface of the pillow.

He tried a wry smile, then said, 'At least we got him, so they tell me.'

'Who told you?' Mary Sullivan sounded cross. 'The doctor specifically ordered that nobody should . . .'

'The doctor.' The smile made another attempt. 'I pestered him a little. *He* told me.'

Steve said, 'Forget the John Doe jerk, Dad. There was a shoot-out. He fell, and was barbecued.'

'We'll never know,' signed Sullivan. He seemed to be talking quietly to himself. 'We'll never know who he was. We'll never know his real name. It's a pity, that. I'd have liked to have . . .'

'Steve's already said.' Mary Sullivan leaned forward and folded her fingers around the hand which rested on the coverlet. 'Forget it, Richard, *please*. Just rest. Get better. Come back home to us. We need you.'

188

Post Scriptum

9.30 p.m.

The scene was enacted at Leeds. It could have been anywhere. The words and music were as old as law-enforcement itself; they'd been originally performed when the first detective sought information from the wife of some tearaway he wished to interview. As old as *that* and, more or less, the same dialogue.

'Where's Ted?'

'Dunno.'

'Now, come *on*, of course you know.'

'Naw. Not for a week or two now.'

'You're his wife.'

'Aye? Tell that to some o' them fancy tarts 'e laikes around wi'.'

'That where he is?'

'I dunno. 'E just pissed off an' left. You know *him*. Some bloody scheme or another, so 'e said. I didn't ask.'

'So where *might* he be?'

' 'Ow the 'ell do I know? I'm nobbut 'is wife. I get told nowt.'

'When he gets back . . .'

' 'E'll find sod-all 'ere for 'im. I've 'ad enough. I've been round to t' welfare bloke. 'E says I can take 'im to court. *Make* the bleeder – worris it? – "meet 'is obligations". Aye. That's it. I can *make* the bleeder meet 'is obligations. An' by Christ I'm gonna.'

'When he comes back, *if* he comes back, give us a wink. We'd like a word with him.'

'Mister, if *'e* comes back – I tell yer . . . I'll murder the bugger.'

Post Post Scriptum

TUESDAY – SEPTEMBER 27th

8.15 a.m.

The letter had puzzled them, at first. The stamp. The postmark. Who did *they* know in Eire? It was addressed to 'Mrs. K. Clarke' and Kim read it aloud to her husband, as they sipped tea and munched toast.

The second page of the letter ran :

'a foolish idea. How near I was to returning home you'll never know. I even reached Bordfield. But good sense took over and I caught the train to Stranraer and, from there, the ferry to Larne.

Crossing the border was ridiculously easy. Far easier than I expected. There are hundreds, literally hundreds, of footpaths, cart tracks and minor roads leading from County Armagh to County Monaghan and once you're in County Monaghan you're here, in Republican Ireland.

I once thought I'd have to go farther afield to find peace. As far as Canada. In fact I toyed with the idea of a place called Moose Jaw. Why Moose Jaw? To be honest, I don't know. The name attracted me. That's the only explanation I can offer. But I was wrong. This place is beautiful. And very peaceful. As I write this I can look out of my window and see the whole of Tralee Bay, with Kerry Head away on my right.

It's a beautiful little cottage, and ridiculously cheap.

I was amazed. And that brings me to the reason for this letter.

By this time, according to my reckoning, Sam will be home. You will, I hope, have signed the papers and moved into the old house. That's why I've addressed this letter to you there. There are no strings attached, Kim. Let me make that quite plain. But if Sam is finding difficulty in getting employment, or if, for any other reason, you feel like selling the house and joining me here, there's a gem of a smallholding, complete with cottage, next to my own. We could, perhaps, combine. We might even buy more land if we prosper. That's something we can talk over if you decide to.'

She ended the letter, and looked across the table at her husband.

Clarke said, 'He's a good man. The best man I ever met.'

'He's my father,' she said, quietly.

Clarke nodded, and said, 'One of the few men who've never done a wrong thing in the whole of his life.